SLEEPING CAT BLUES

THE CLEVER CAT MYSTERIES
BOOK 6

ALISON O'LEARY

Print ISBN: 978-1-916978-93-5

For Eddie

CHAPTER ONE

The headstones stood straight and smart, their shiny black surfaces barely touched by time and weather. The graves they guarded, decades old, held small pots of fresh flowers. Deep inscriptions, etched in gold lettering, told the tale of lives lost almost before they had begun. The woman glanced around her and then rose from her knees. She pulled her coat collar more tightly around her face and walked quickly away. The occupants of the graves lay sleeping, unaware that she had visited once more.

Jeremy watched as a small funeral procession made its slow progress along the road. A modest affair with a simple floral tribute and just one car following. He wondered who it was. Given the small number of mourners, probably not a young person. When a young person died, their friends and classmates turned out in droves, their teenage faces frozen in appalled disbelief that one of their number had actually ceased to exist, their voices stunned into silence at the thought that they would never see them again. So, no, this definitely wasn't a young person's funeral. They had a number of elderly neighbours though, some of whom had been here for years. It was probably one of them.

That was the trouble with having his study at the front of the house, Jeremy thought. At the time, the small bedroom over the porch had seemed ideal but now he wasn't so sure. Too close to the window, too many distractions. He turned away from the view of the street and looked at his desk. The papers he had been working on earlier lay scattered across the surface. So much to do. Inspection reports to write, visits to arrange, training to attend and so very little inclination to do any of it. Settling back down in his chair, he re-read the last sentence that he'd written. *While acknowledging difficulties in staffing, it is evident that in some areas the school has yet to demonstrate...*

He sighed. Yet to demonstrate what exactly? Demonstrate that they were slightly above the shite category into which he had mentally placed them on his recent inspection visit? That would be the honest answer. But short of sticking a bundle of dynamite under it, changing its name and starting again somewhere else, he wasn't entirely sure what the school could do about it. Situated in a semi-rural area with poor public transport links, high house prices and little to do by way of recreation, the chances of attracting quality teaching staff were remote to say the least. And, according to the head, the school budget had been cut in real terms year on year. It was all very well telling them that they had to improve, but if they didn't have the tools to do it, it was pretty much a lost cause. Might as well enter a one-legged man in an arse-kicking contest.

He dropped his forehead into his hands. He didn't know what was the matter with him lately. He had a constant feeling of restlessness, an inability to settle, which was most unlike him. By and large he had always been content with his lot. He wouldn't have said that he was complacent but in truth he had pretty much everything he wanted. A nice home, sufficient income, a wife that he loved dearly and, for the past few years, a foster son, Carlos, of whom he had grown deeply fond. Some of those poor sods sleeping on the streets would think they were in heaven if they had only a tenth of what he had, and he knew it. But recently he had experienced a strange kind of yearning, a reaching for something, but what that something was he didn't know. A bit like Mole in *The Wind in the Willows*. What was it that Mole had said? Something about 'Bother' and 'O blow' and 'Hang spring cleaning!' and he had bolted out of the house without even waiting to put on his coat. Except that Jeremy didn't have any spring cleaning. And he didn't want to bolt out of the house, with or without his coat. He just wanted... what?

He swivelled round in his chair and let his arms fall down behind him. Tipping his head back, he gazed up at the bookshelves and spotted Aubrey slumped, eyes fast shut, tail hanging down. He grinned. That feline air of studied innocence didn't fool him. The rascal must have snuck in when he went to the bathroom. He'd already chucked him out twice this afternoon for messing about with the cables behind his desk. Ah well. Might as well let him stay there now. He was a good old boy, by and large. Except when he wasn't.

He spun back round to face the door as Molly put her head round it.

"What time are you coming down?"

"Any minute now." He shifted his gaze back to his laptop and logged off. He really wasn't going to do any more this afternoon and it was no use pretending that he was. "I've just about finished for the day."

Molly crossed the room and looked out of the window. The funeral procession had just reached the end of the road and was turning right.

"That's probably Mrs Ross. I heard that she died."

Jeremy looked up from his desk, surprised.

"Did you know her then?"

"Not really. Her nephew brought her to Lilac Tree Lodge to have a look round." Molly smiled suddenly. "It was obvious that he was wasting his time. I could tell just by looking at her that she had no intention of coming to live there, she was just humouring him. I knew that she lived on our road, so I called in to see her afterwards. Just to make sure that she had everything she needed."

"What was she like?" Jeremy asked, suddenly curious. He had seen the old lady out and about at various times, although he had never spoken to her. He wished now that he had. It wouldn't have killed him to pass the time of day with her.

Aubrey opened one eye. He knew Mrs Ross, although she was more Vincent's mate than his. But she was a good old sort. Didn't make a fuss that day when they slipped in through an open window and she found them sitting on one of the kitchen worktops. In fact, she'd smiled and given them a small tin of tuna to share while she told them what she'd watched on television last night. Aubrey had the impression that she didn't see many people.

Molly considered Jeremy's question for a moment.

"Nice. Friendly. But nobody's fool, if you know what I mean. I was a bit worried that she'd think I was interfering but she asked me in for a cup of tea and we had a chat. I got the feeling that she didn't get many visitors."

"Not the nephew?"

Molly shook her head.

"I don't think so. All the time they were at the Lodge, he kept checking his phone and looking at his watch. He clearly had better things to do."

"How old was she?"

Molly thought for a moment.

"Difficult to tell. In her eighties maybe?"

"Why did the nephew take her to the Lodge? Didn't she have anyone else?"

"No. There was a daughter but she died years ago. There was a framed photograph of her on the mantlepiece, Mrs Ross pointed it out to me. It must have been taken sometime in the seventies by the look of it. A pretty girl, she looked about nine or ten."

"How did she die? Was it an accident or something?"

Molly shook her head.

"No. She was murdered."

CHAPTER TWO

J eremy hesitated slightly and then strode into the classroom. The desks were arranged in a horseshoe. No chance of following his teenage instinct and sliding in at the back then. At the front, a small woman with greying hair scrunched up on top of her head was fiddling with papers and tapping at the keyboard of the small laptop that sat on the desk. Jeremy watched for a moment as she frowned up at the big white screen attached to the wall. They were obviously in for some visuals. What would she think, Jeremy wondered, if she knew that he was an Ofsted inspector? But for tonight, he suddenly realised, he wasn't. Tonight he was just another student. One of a class of six who had signed up for a series of open lectures on the town's history, given by the local history society and hosted free of charge by the college as part of its community participation programme.

He took a seat and looked around him. He still wasn't quite sure what he was doing here. History, local or otherwise, wasn't something that he'd often given any real thought to, other than to watch a documentary on the television now and then, and occasionally pausing to glance over the names on the war memorial in the town centre. But Molly, sensing his low mood and recent restlessness, had pointed the advert out to him in the local paper and he had been surprised at how seriously he was tempted. In fact, so seriously tempted that he'd signed up for it. They'd lived in the town for quite a while now and he still didn't really know much about the place. Besides, it would be something to do, something different. It would get him out of the house. Out of his study and away from his computer.

He cast a furtive look at his classmates. Three older women and two other men. Surprisingly low number given that the class was free, but perhaps everybody had just got used to doing things online now. What, he wondered, had made this lot turn out? Were they, like him, restless and looking for something new to do? Were they lonely? Bored? Or maybe they had a genuine interest in the subject. He fiddled with the A4 pad that he'd brought with him, jotting down the date at the top of the first page while he slid a glance further along. The women, seated to the right of the centre, clearly knew one another. Elderly women, he realised suddenly, had changed. The old stereotypes of his youth were well and truly outdated. No longer the white-haired old biddy in the cosy slippers who was as round as she was tall and always had a sweet or two in her pinny pocket for the grandkids, or the hatchet-faced old cow with the claw-like hands and vinegar tongue beloved of sixties television drama. Nowadays old women had smart haircuts and well-cut clothes. They painted their nails and they had opinions. They didn't fade into the background with an apologetic air for existing.

He watched them as they chatted easily together, fishing about in their bags, pulling out notebooks and pens. What had drawn them to this particular event, he wondered. Perhaps they were serial evening class attendees, working their way mob-handed through the gamut of adult education classes offered by the local schools and college. They should get loyalty points. He shook his thoughts free and sat up, prepared to concentrate, as the lecturer straightened her notes and began to speak.

He pulled off his overcoat and flung it over the banister. Molly had lit the fire, he could smell the comforting fragrance from where he was standing. Winter might be over but there was still a chill in the air and an open fire was a nice thing to come home to. Carlos looked up from his phone as he came in.

"How did it go?" asked Molly.

Leaning over and grabbing Aubrey from his place by the fire, Jeremy hauled him onto his lap as he sat down. Aubrey made a mild pretence at resistance and then settled himself. His two favourite resting places were Carlos's bed and Jeremy's lap. He'd even discovered how to turn on Carlos's electric blanket when he'd jumped down one day and landed straight on the controls. It was a trick that he had shared with Vincent, and which both now used to full effect. Stretched along the arm of the chair where Molly was sitting, Vincent lay with his eyes half-closed.

Jeremy reached for the glass of wine that Molly passed him and studied it for a moment before answering.

"Very good. I enjoyed it, more than I expected really. The college is nicer than it looks from the outside."

Which was, thought Aubrey, an understatement. He'd followed Carlos to college one day out of curiosity. The building, mostly glass and concrete, looked more like somewhere you'd get banged up than go to learn something. Inside, however, it was warm and bright and welcoming, with smiley-faced receptionists and comfortable chairs to sit in if you were kept waiting for someone. Aubrey knew they were comfortable because he'd sat in one of them and they hadn't even chucked him out, although he knew that they'd seen him.

Carlos gave a half-smile.

"Yeah, it's all right."

Now in the second year of his catering course, Carlos thought that it was more than all right. Unlike school, where to be different was a clear invitation to have your head kicked in on a regular basis, at college everybody seemed to be different in one way or another. They took a positive pride in it because to be like everybody else was, well, just about the worst thing. Ever. He wasn't sure how he was different, other than that his mother had been murdered and he lived with foster parents. It wasn't the sort of difference he wanted to parade, but, be that as it may, he was really enjoying his time there. In fact, unlike some of his fellow students, he would actually be sorry to leave. Except that when he did leave, he could start on the next leg of his journey, which was to gain experience in restaurants with a view to eventually opening one of his own. Which he would share with Teddy when she finished her A levels and degree. At the thought of Teddy, his heart gave a little squeeze, as it always did. He wondered what she was doing now. Homework probably, or fighting with her brother Casper. He'd WhatsApp her later.

"How many were in the class?" asked Molly.

Jeremy took a mouthful of wine and thought for a moment.

"Six altogether. Three women and three men, including myself. The women looked as though they were retired."

"Did you speak to any of them?"

"We had a short break halfway through and I chatted to one of the other blokes there. Nice chap. Mike. He lost his wife a couple of years ago. It was really sad."

"How did she die? Was she ill?"

"No. A car accident. One of those freak things. She was

turning right and a van just ploughed into her. The driver didn't see her. Apparently he was on his phone," he added.

"Did they have children?" Molly asked.

"Three. All grown up and left home."

For a moment they both fell silent. Aubrey looked at them. As he knew only too well, the curtain between life and death was so very thin, never more so than when it came to unnatural causes. Turn this way and survive. Turn that way and die.

"What was the lecturer like?" said Molly at last.

"She was pretty good. She obviously knows her stuff. She's called Margaret. She's retired now, but she used to be a reporter on one of the London dailies. She teaches evening classes now. Literature, local history, stuff like that."

"What sort of things did she cover?"

"How the town developed, the coming of the railways, how it turned into a holiday resort, that sort of thing. So, did you know for instance, that originally going to the seaside was something that doctors prescribed for their patients? It was supposed to be a cure for things like skin complaints and diseases like gout."

"Gout?" Carlos looked confused. "I thought that was, like, Henry the eighth and all his legs and that."

Jeremy grinned.

"He only had two, Carlos."

"People still get gout now," said Molly. "Some of the residents at Lilac Tree Lodge suffer from it. It's very painful."

"Anyway," continued Jeremy, hastily heading off what he could see was about to become a major side-track from Carlos, "the town sort of grew from there. Visiting the seaside became fashionable. And of course, once it became fashionable there was money to be made. Quite a lot of money, it seems. For instance, piers that were originally just built as simple wooden landing stages for boats grew into entertainment venues. They started putting on shows and opening booths selling food and drink. Margaret showed us some photographs taken in about 1920. It looked a riot."

Carlos stared at him doubtfully. Their local pier didn't look much like an entertainment venue to him. Long and straggling, it looked like a rusty old finger pointing out to sea. The only things on it were a couple of old slot machines that had long since been vandalised, and a few broken benches.

Jeremy looked at the expression on his face and smiled.

"Remember, that was before television and cinema. In those days people took their fun where they could. Life was simpler then." He paused for a second and then added, "Albeit usually shorter. Anyway, at the end Margaret asked if anybody had any questions, and Mike asked if there had been any notable crimes in the area."

Carlos leaned forward, interested.

"What, like murders and that?"

Jeremy nodded.

"Yes, like murders and that. There was one particularly horrific murder of a police constable back in 1900. He was beaten by some drunks outside the Mistletoe Hotel on a freezing winter night and left to die. Nobody came to help him."

Molly looked horrified.

"Why not?"

Jeremy shrugged.

"I guess they didn't like him. He was called Cornelius Bennett and he's buried in St Andrew's churchyard. I might go and pay him a visit the next time I'm out for a walk. And then there was the Victorian wife, Alma something, who poisoned her husband. There seems to have been quite a fashion for poisoning husbands at the time, although there was talk in the town that in this case the accused might have been innocent."

"Did people think that someone else had given him the poison?" asked Carlos.

"Possibly. But there was a suggestion that he might have taken it himself," said Jeremy. "Some people did in those days, they thought that it was a kind of stimulus or tonic."

Carlos looked horrified.

"What? Like taking vitamins?"

"I suppose so. According to Margaret, the widow wasn't without friends. Apparently her husband was a right bast..." He paused and checked himself. He'd been a bit too free with the language lately. He didn't want Carlos thinking that it was okay for everyday use. "So and so," he continued. "There must have been some sympathy for her anyway, because she wasn't sentenced to hang. She went to prison. Apparently she was released after thirty years and she lived until she was ninety-three."

He fell silent for a moment.

"Anything else?" asked Molly.

"Well, yes." Jeremy spoke slowly, his expression grave. "She told us about a series of murders that took place in the seventies. The police never found the person responsible."

CHAPTER THREE

____

Jeremy paused and took another sip of his wine. When Margaret had told them about the unfortunate policeman, they had all been interested and engaged. And when she had talked about what had seemed like a positive tidal wave of Victorian women poisoning their husbands they had been both appalled and thrilled in equal measure. But when she had talked about the seventies murders, something in the room had changed. He couldn't quite put his finger on what it was but the atmosphere had altered. It was as if the temperature had dropped. Coming from somewhere near the middle of the room, it had spread outwards until it had felt as though everybody had suddenly started holding their breath, including him. Perhaps because the other murders that Margaret had talked about were like stories out of a history book, something from the dim and distant past. Whereas the 1970s, well, that was a bit closer to home. All the people in the class had lived through them. And the victims that she talked about had been children.

"They were called the 'golf course murders'," said Jeremy. "Because that's where the bodies were found. Well, two of them were found near the golf course." He pulled a face. "Where I play. There's a piece of wasteland, a kind of no-man's land, that butts on to the eastern edge. It's still there now. I don't know who owns it. Not the golf club. But it's pretty overgrown, mostly shrubs and weeds. Two girls had gone missing and were eventually found in an old underground air raid shelter."

Carlos paused scrolling his phone and looked up.

"A what?"

"An air raid shelter. It's where people used to go to shelter from the bombs during the Second World War."

"What, and they're still there?"

Jeremy nodded.

"Most of them, I think. I suppose because they're underground people just forgot about them. I guess that once the war was over people just wanted to get on with their lives, and there were more pressing things to do than seal up some air raid shelters. So they just stayed. There was one on the playing fields of my school, right up at the top."

"Could you get into it?" Carlos asked, curious.

"Oh yes. There were some steps down that led you in, lots of the kids played down there although I don't suppose their parents knew. I expect that's what the girls were doing. I used to go down to the one at my school with my mates and drink cider in the school holidays."

Carlos looked impressed.

"Who found them?" asked Molly. "I mean, presumably most people had forgotten that the shelter was there."

"I guess that was what the murderer was relying on," said Jeremy. "People got together to help the police and formed search parties. They looked in all the likely places, parks and playgrounds and so on, and then somebody remembered the waste ground by the golf course."

"You said two of them," said Molly. "Does that mean that there were more?"

"One more," said Jeremy. "A little boy. His body was found later, round the back of the clubhouse. Margaret gave us all the details because she's been researching it for a book she's writing. It was a huge story at the time. It hit all the national press."

Carlos interrupted, his eyes alight and his expression suddenly eager.

"It happened one summer in the school holidays, back in the old days."

Jeremy stared at him, surprised.

"How do you know?"

"I think it's the same one we were talking about it in the common room the other week. Carrie said that her mum told her about it. All these kids got killed. Carrie said that her mum was only little at the time but everybody was really afraid. Like, none of the kids were allowed to go out and play and it was really hard because it was the school holidays. And when her older sister went to youth club, her dad had to take her there and pick her up."

Jeremy nodded.

"I'm not surprised. When you think about the reality of it, the whole thing must have been like some kind of living nightmare," he said. "The murders themselves, obviously, but also the impact that it had on people living there at the time. Margaret said that it affected everyone, there was a real atmosphere of fear hanging over the town. Everybody was looking at everybody else and wondering and it didn't help that at that time of year there were lots of holidaymakers as well. She said she had just started her first job and she was sent down here with a senior reporter to cover the story."

"And the police never caught whoever did it?" asked Molly.

Jeremy shook his head.

"No. They thought they had at first. A local man was arrested and confessed."

"What happened?"

"It went to court and he was sentenced. But he was released later on appeal."

"That was what Carrie's mum told her," said Carlos. "She said that the bloke that got arrested was called Harvey and he was always hanging around the ice-cream vans and that, and wanting to play with the local kids even though he was, like, grown-up and everything. But it turned out in the end that he didn't do it so they had to let him out of prison. Carrie's mum said that he didn't have a fair trial." He paused. "What does that mean? Was it, like, they were prejudiced against him because he was a bit..."

He paused and shot a sideways glance at Molly. What words were they allowed to use nowadays? He had been going to say, was it because he was a bit backward but that didn't sound right. He'd heard adults describing children as being too forward as well, and that apparently wasn't a good thing either. So if they couldn't be backward and they couldn't be forward, what should they be? No doubt he'd work it out when he was old, like twenty-five or something. In the meantime, what were the correct words to describe Harvey? When he was little his mother, along with many others of her generation, had always used the word 'mental' but he had the distinct feeling that wouldn't be acceptable either.

The sound of his mother's voice, never too far away, drifted into his consciousness.

"So you see, Carlos. Some people, they are mental. Mental people cannot help what they do, so we must remember that and we must always be kind to them."

Although, he reflected, she hadn't been so kind to the big boy who had grabbed his toy truck from him when he was about five. As he recalled, in spite of the fact that the boy was clearly what his mother would have described as 'mental', she had threatened to beat the shit out of him.

Jeremy looked at him and smiled. He knew exactly what Carlos was thinking. He had a face like an open book.

"I don't think that there was a trial as such," he said. "Because he told the police that he'd done it."

"So, what, like they didn't have a jury or anything?"

"I'm not sure, but I don't think so. I think if somebody admits that they've done it, it goes straight to sentencing. Which in the case of murder would be life imprisonment."

"So how did he get out?"

"From what I gather, questions were raised later about his confession," Jeremy said. "Margaret said that there was some issues over how the police interviews were conducted, and whether in fact he really understood what he was confessing to."

"Surely he had some kind of legal representation. Didn't he have a solicitor present?" asked Molly.

"I think so but there were questions about how long it took him to get there. And by the time he arrived, Harvey had already confessed."

"Surely the solicitor would have at least raised a question?"

Jeremy shrugged.

"According to Margaret, the solicitor wasn't particularly interested. So no, apparently not."

"Why though?" asked Carlos. "Why did he confess if he didn't do it?"

Aubrey, who had been listening with interest, agreed. Catch him or Vincent owning up to... well, anything really. Never mind something that they hadn't done. It was one of the first rules of cat law. Keep your trap shut and look innocent. He thought suddenly of Conker, the little russet-coloured cat that had lived in their old neighbourhood. Conker, unlike the rest of the mob, was the sort who confessed before he was accused, to the extent that none of the other cats took him seriously. Which was how he had got away for so long with raiding the emergency supplies that the cats kept in an abandoned shed on the allotments. In fact, now he thought about it, Conker wasn't nearly as stupid as he looked. Which was just as well. He pricked his ears as Jeremy continued talking.

"Who knows?" Jeremy looked thoughtful. "Some people do confess to crimes that they haven't committed."

Carlos raised his eyebrows.

"I still don't get it. Why? Why would anybody go around saying that they've done something when they haven't?"

"To feel important, I suppose" said Jeremy. "To put themselves at the centre of attention. Although I didn't get the impression that was the reason Harvey confessed. From the way Margaret described it, it sounded like he didn't really understand what he was being asked. It was as though he thought that if he just said he'd done whatever they were asking him about then he could go home and have his tea. That, and the fact that they had no real evidence other than general suspicion, it meant that there was sufficient grounds to make his conviction unsafe. I think that about the only thing they had on him was that he was often seen on the golf course."

"What, he played golf?"

Carlos looked amazed.

Jeremy smiled.

"No, he looked for lost golf balls. Especially on the wasteland, the odd ball gets hit over there even now. The club members used to give him a couple of bob for each one he found."

Carlos nodded. That made more sense. He wasn't sure what a couple of bob was but it was probably, like, old speak for pounds or something.

"Why did he get sent to prison then if there wasn't any proper evidence?"

"As I said, he confessed," said Jeremy. "Which meant that there wasn't a requirement for a full trial and so the evidence, or lack of it, was never put to the test. Years later, long after Harvey was released, the golf course murders came up in a cold-case review and somebody had the bright idea of checking for DNA on some of the clothing that they'd kept in storage. "

"Why didn't they do that in the first place?" asked Carlos. "Then Harvey wouldn't have had to go to prison."

"Science wasn't so advanced at the time the murders happened. It wasn't like it is now. People didn't know about DNA in those days. It was still methods like taking fingerprints."

"Whose clothes did they test?" asked Molly. "Harvey's or the victims'?"

"Both," said Jeremy. "As well as a couple of strands of hair caught in a little necklace that one of the girls was wearing, and which had been kept along with the clothing. But there was no match with Harvey. It seemed to prove fairly conclusively that it wasn't him. But the police never arrested anybody else."

"What about the little boy?" asked Molly.

"Apparently most of the evidence relating to him was nowhere to be found. Probably languishing somewhere in some long-forgotten basement. The only thing that they had was the file made at the time which included a note of his blood group, which was AB negative, and they did track down his parents and persuade them to let them have some of his things which they tested, just so they'd have a note of his DNA. Not that they could do much with it," he added.

"Why not?" asked Carlos. "I mean, once they had all the DNA and that, why couldn't they find the real killer?"

Jeremy shrugged.

"Because they didn't have anybody to test it against. Which I guess means that the real killer's DNA wasn't in the system."

Carlos frowned.

"Isn't everybody's?"

"No. I think that it's only taken if you're arrested or charged with a crime or something."

Carlos looked thoughtful. His father had been in prison. More than once. Did that mean that his DNA was in the system? Another thought struck him. He didn't know much about genetics but if his father's DNA was in the system, perhaps that meant that his own was as well. But that was in Brazil. Maybe they had a different system there. He pushed the thought away. He had no intention of committing any crime, so it didn't matter really.

"The victims, were they..."

Molly hesitated and her eyes met Jeremy's. Carlos wasn't a child anymore. In fact, he could probably tell them a thing or two. But somehow it felt wrong to talk about such things in front of him. She glanced across at his dark head bent over his phone again. For all that he'd been through in his short life, in many respects he was still such an innocent.

Jeremy shook his head.

"Apparently not."

"Did Margaret say how they were killed?" she asked.

"The girls were strangled. The boy was stabbed. Margaret said that there was some peculiarity about the weapon. It was a kind of knife but not anything like an ordinary kitchen one. It was something unusual but they couldn't say what. They never found it anyway. Margaret said that the police were fairly sure that the boy had been killed somewhere else and taken there afterwards."

"How did that happen without anybody seeing?" Carlos sounded incredulous.

"I should think," said Jeremy, "that whoever it was that killed him, took the boy there after dark and almost certainly by car. Margaret said that was one of the things that would have been difficult to explain if Harvey had stood full trial. The poor bloke could just about walk and talk at the same time. He certainly couldn't drive."

"So wouldn't somebody have noticed a car pulling up by the bins? Somebody in the restaurant, I mean?" asked Molly.

Jeremy shook his head.

"No. In those days, although the restaurant did lunches every day, they didn't do evening meals unless it was for a special function. A couple of members were talking about it the other week. At that time there would have been nobody in the restaurant to see anything."

"Cameras?" suggested Molly.

"Remember, this is the seventies that we're talking about. There were almost certainly no surveillance cameras or anything then. Or now, probably," he added. "I mean, what's the point? They're only bins. Who'd want to steal anything from a bin?"

Aubrey shot a quick glance across at Vincent, who opened one eye and gave a slight grin. What kind of question was that? Who would want to steal anything from a bin? They would, for a start. They both liked a good bin. It was amazing how much food people threw out. Once they had found a slab of roast beef, just chucked in with all the other rubbish. There was no doubt about it, there was nothing like a successful bin scavenge to make their day. They didn't actually need to do it, they had plenty to eat, but it was as well to keep your paw in.

Carlos looked thoughtful. Life must have been really weird back in the old days. Molly had told him only recently that nobody had remotes. So if you wanted to change the channel on the television you had to actually get up and press a switch or something. They must have been permanently exhausted. And according to Jeremy, you could go carting bodies around and nobody noticed. They didn't even have mobiles either. Or the internet. It was a wonder that they didn't all go mad. Or perhaps they did. Perhaps all that getting up and down and changing television channels drove them that way, and that was why they carted bodies around in the dark.

"Anyway," continued Jeremy. "It was an interesting evening, I'm glad I went."

He paused and thought for a moment. What was it that Margaret had said just before the class finished? Something about having just discovered some new line of enquiry, some new lead that she had heard about that very day which, if it came to anything, would blow the whole case wide open again. She hadn't said what it was though. He smiled slightly. It was probably a hook to get them to buy her book when it came out.

CHAPTER FOUR

Across the other side of town, the woman fished in her handbag for her door keys while Clara tried to weave in and out of her ankles. She reached down and stroked her soft little head. Poor thing. She was getting so old. Even the effort of purring seemed to exhaust her. Without pausing to shrug off her coat, she made straight for the kitchen. Tipping the contents of the wet food pouch into Clara's bowl, she stood back and watched her for a moment. She felt a sudden lump rise to her throat. The last of a litter of kittens that had belonged to her brother, Clara had been her constant companion for almost twenty years and she could hardly bear the thought of losing her.

Many a long night she had sat up late in bed with Clara nestled beside her, flicking the remote at the television and watching anything that came up, trying to stave off the time when she would fall asleep. She still dreaded, even now, after all these years, the ghastly dreams that tiptoed into her subconscious and shook her, sweating and afraid, into wakefulness. The dreams that made her reach instinctively for the soft warm body of the little cat curled up next to her. But

Clara couldn't, she knew, last for much longer. It was odd, she thought, how when a pet died almost the first thing that people said was, will you get another one. They didn't say it about husbands and wives. She sighed. Right now, Clara was the least of her worries. She had more pressing things to think about. She turned away and pulled open the fridge door.

The supermarket can of gin and tonic was ready and waiting. With one sharp tug she ripped off the tab and, without bothering to find a glass, took a large gulp. God, that felt good. She wasn't a big drinker but there were definitely times when only a slug of alcohol would do, and tonight was one of them. She walked slowly through to the sitting room, flicked on the lamp, and sank down on the sofa. Leaning back, she felt the alcohol work its magic as the tension started to drain from her body. She closed her eyes and let her head rest against the big soft cushions. She needed to think.

That it might have been raised had never even crossed her mind. If it had, she wouldn't have signed up for the class. Of that she was sure. She would have made her excuses to the others, pretended that she didn't fancy it or something, and then just ignored it. But it simply hadn't occurred to her. Not for a single second. Why would it? In recent years she had managed to bury it so successfully that it only re-emerged in nightmares. If it ever did resurface during waking hours it was something from the distant past, like one of the old black and white movies that she had watched on rainy Sunday afternoons when she was young. It was nothing to do with her. And now, as a result of a simple question innocently asked, it was slowly clambering out of the darkness and groping its way into the clear daylight of her consciousness like some evil velvet-skinned mole. She opened her eyes again and stared at the wall. That damned woman, Margaret, had said that she was writing a book about it. But, what was even worse, she was claiming to have some new lead on the case. Was that possible? After all this time? It couldn't be. Could it?

She felt a dull thump of pain blunder across her forehead and settle behind her left eye. A sure sign of the forerunner to anxiety, the deep formless pit into which she occasionally sank, the unwelcome residue of events long past. But this time it wasn't some vague foreboding that she couldn't pin down. This time it was real. This time she had something to be anxious about. She rubbed at her forehead with her free hand, the other still clutching the can of drink. Of course, she had known as soon as the word *crime* was uttered what was coming. It was inevitable. How could the subject of crime in the town be discussed and the golf course murders not be at the top of the list? Tiny icicles of fear had started forming at the back of her mind, and her hands and feet had felt suddenly cold. She had sat stony-faced, staring straight ahead of her, listening to the stories of dead policemen and Victorian poisoners while she waited with a growing sense of dread for what she knew was coming. And come it had.

The whole dreadful story had been unravelled before them like some ghastly tapestry, each detail unfurled for their entertainment. Margaret had obviously done her research, and done it thoroughly. She had even known the name of the solicitor that had represented Harvey, the poor local halfwit that the police had taken in for questioning. As she sipped at her drink, the memories of that summer, squeezed into the dark crevices of her mind for so long, suddenly burst out and hit her full on, billowing up with such force that it almost knocked the breath from her. She could taste the very air.

There had been an unexpected heatwave that month. It had brought a rush of summer visitors to the town, with the result that the hotels and guest houses had been full and the sound of people enjoying themselves in the local pubs and restaurants had throbbed out into the hot night air. The pier had still been a real tourist attraction then, instead of the eyesore that it was now, and people had made the most of it. They had enjoyed themselves in much the same way as their Victorian forebears had done, promenading up and down and buying ice creams and candy floss from the little stalls strung along the length of it. There had even been a Punch and Judy show and the children, like generations before them, had laughed innocently at the antics of the puppets. Antics which, these days, might well be considered decidedly dark. In the little theatre next to the pier there had been what the promoters billed as summer specials, featuring faces from television and the music world. That summer it had seemed that the sun never stopped shining and everybody was happy. Until the children had been reported missing.

Their presence had been confirmed by police dogs gathered barking around the entrance to the air raid shelter where the girls had lain, small and broken, thrown down like abandoned dolls. Any pretence that they would turn up safe and sound, that they were simply playing somewhere or had strayed too far from home and managed to get themselves lost, disappeared. The happy carefree feeling that had prevailed for most of the summer had been snuffed out and replaced by one of fear and dread. The normally placid townsfolk had turned a cold and critical eye on the police.

Located in an inconspicuous, dimly-lit building on the edge of town, the local force up until that point had been generally low-key. The age of taking bobbies off the beat and sending them out in cars instead had already started and the police were rarely seen unless it was to attend an accident on the newly-built bypass or break up an after-hours fight in the town's small nightclub. Now that changed. Suddenly the police were everywhere, both uniformed and plain-clothed, and people fell over themselves to answer their questions. Local radio and television stations went into overdrive demanding answers and there was much talk of 'bringing in the Yard' or at the very least co-opting help from neighbouring counties.

When the third child was reported as missing and his body found two days later, the levels of hysteria had soared almost to melting point. An undersized child, he had been discovered, not in the air raid shelter on the wasteland, but lying face down behind the bins at the back of the golf club restaurant, the jagged knife wound in his back exposed to the air. As a result, the atmosphere had become febrile, the nervous tension rising with the thermometer until it had become almost unbearable. The very air had seemed to press down, smothering people with panic and fear. Rumour and speculation had run rife, and many of the visitors, particularly those with children, cut short their holiday and fled to the safety of their own homes.

Neighbour had begun to look at neighbour with sharp-eyed sideways glances, shooting poisoned darts of suspicion that left their venomous trails for years to come. There had been more than one anonymous call to the police naming potential suspects and every man, young and old, had come under scrutiny. The town had become more or less deserted as people stayed behind closed doors, only venturing out when strictly necessary. The children, who in the school holidays would normally be found playing in the streets and parks, were nowhere to be seen. It was as though the Pied Piper of Hamelin had danced through the town and led them all away. The whole area had come to a virtual standstill and, after two weeks, the police had still seemed no closer to tracking the killer.

Harvey's arrest had come as a surprise and there had been more than one person in the town who suspected that in the absence of anybody else of interest, the police had homed in on Harvey as the most likely to offer the least resistance. Well-known around the neighbourhood and generally regarded as harmless, his shambling presence was known to most, if not all, of the townspeople. He had been regarded as pretty much a fixture, in much the same way as the statue of Sir George Renton, a local benefactor, in the town square. A solid man in his late twenties with thick shoulders, large hands and an open loose-lipped grin, Harvey had the mental age of a five-year-old. In the days when children were beginning to be warned about stranger danger, it had always been felt that there was nothing to fear from Harvey. Apart from anything else, he wasn't a stranger. Everybody knew him and it would have been difficult to find anybody who wished him any harm. But that didn't stop many people from breathing a collective sigh of secret guilty relief when he was taken into custody. The general feeling had been that, in spite of reservations, at last the police were actually doing something.

For her, Harvey's arrest had been a godsend. He had been the perfect fall guy. She had even tried to persuade herself that, as far as Harvey was concerned, it was actually all for the best. After all, what kind of life lay ahead of him on the outside? In spite of being strong and healthy, he was intellectually incapable of any sort of work and his drug-addled mother that he lived with couldn't last for much longer. Most days it was about all she could do to drag her wasted skeletal frame out of bed. But at least their combined state benefits kept a roof over their heads and gave them sufficient money to buy food, which Harvey purchased from the local shops with the aid of a list which she scrawled out for him to hand over to the shopkeeper. What would happen to Harvey when he was left on his own?

He couldn't manage by himself, that was for sure. At least if he was in prison Harvey would be clothed and fed. He would be looked after and cared for. And he might not even go to prison. They might find him guilty and then take him to some kind of institution. Which was surely the best outcome, for all concerned.

When the murders had stopped, the mood in the town had lightened as people had begun to believe that the police must have picked up the right man after all. Except her. She didn't think that the police had picked up the right man. She knew only too well that they hadn't.

CHAPTER FIVE

Jeremy lifted his face to the watery sunshine, closed his eyes, and inhaled through his nostrils. He'd gone a bit large on the red wine last night and the feeling of the sharp spring air filling his lungs was just what he needed to help clear his head. But that aside, the feeling of being outside on this lovely day, away from his laptop and away from reports and endless updates, raised his spirits. He loved his work, of course he did, it was the kind of job that he'd always wanted, but of late it had seemed that he spent far more time staring at a screen than he did going out to visit schools and colleges. The truth was that he missed the contact with other people and he missed the buzz of stepping into a new situation. He even missed the old nervous anticipation that he'd sometimes experienced in his teaching days, that dry-mouthed tension of half-expecting a mini riot from Year Ten simply because it was Monday. It had been at least a month since his last inspection visit and apart from attending the local history lecture, the only people he had spoken to were Molly and Carlos. The luxury of being able to sit around in his old jeans and drink endless mugs of coffee while he was working was starting to wear decidedly thin.

Ahead of him, Aubrey and Vincent mooched through the undergrowth, pausing now and again to look back and check that he was still there. He liked it that the cats had started following him on his daily walks, there was something companiable about it. Molly had been concerned at first, worried about roads and traffic, but as he had said to her, short of locking them in, he couldn't stop them following him if he wanted to. Anyway, he didn't want to. They were free to come and go through the cat flap and this was a quiet residential area. The roads around their house were pretty free of cars during the daytime. And it wasn't as if they would be roaming for miles. He never went further than the small park at the top of the road or over to St Andrew's, the pretty early Victorian church that was situated about half a mile in the other direction, which was where he was headed today.

Navigating the spreading roots of a yew tree, Aubrey came to a halt and turned to Vincent.

"Do you think he's all right?"

Vincent flicked his paw over his ear and gave it a quick wash. Economical as ever with words, he thought for a moment.

"Probably."

Both cats gazed steadily at Jeremy. Lately, they had agreed, he hadn't been quite himself. There had been something almost melancholic about him. His usual good-natured temperament had seemed slightly dimmed and for several days now he had forgotten to dip his hand into the cat treats for them when he went downstairs for coffee. Molly and Carlos had both noticed it too, with Molly making him his favourite shepherd's pie for dinner more often, while Carlos had found some early paperback editions of Jeremy's beloved Agatha Christie online and had presented them to him on his birthday with a flourish. Jeremy had been pleased with the books but he hadn't, both Aubrey and Vincent noticed, actually opened them. He hadn't even ticked them off on his list of wanted Agatha Christie publications. He had simply placed them with the rest of his collection on the bookshelf.

Unaware of the scrutiny from Aubrey and Vincent, Jeremy looked around him. Away to the west a group of workmen were moving some old graves, carefully stacking the headstones against the wall. Small figures in the distance, etched against the blue spring sky, they looked like a medieval engraving. There was, he thought, something very peaceful about a churchyard, particularly one that was overgrown like this one was. Somebody had pushed some daffodil bulbs into the earth along the edge of the path and their bright trumpets nodded and swayed slightly in the breeze. There would be some comfort in being laid to rest in this place. It was where Margaret had said that Cornelius Bennett, the poor murdered police officer, was buried. Perhaps he could try and find him while he was here. He would be interested to know what it said on the headstone, assuming that he had one of course. Not everybody did, he knew. But assuming that somebody had cared enough to cough up for one, would it say anything about how he had died? Was that allowed? He knew that local authority cemeteries were pretty strict about what could and couldn't be placed on graves, including what was written on the headstone, but he wasn't sure about church graveyards. And now he thought about it, he didn't think that he'd ever seen the cause of death on one, not that he'd made a study of it. It would be interesting if it said something Gothic and menacing, like *'foully murdered'* or *'cruelly beaten and left to die'*, but he thought it unlikely. It would probably be something ambiguous like *'taken too soon'* or *'left us too early'*. Anyway, when he found it he'd take a photograph on his phone to show Molly and Carlos.

Slipping his reading glasses from his jacket pocket, he stooped over the nearest stone.

"Morning, Jeremy."

Jeremy jumped. The only time there were people in the churchyard on a weekday was when there was a funeral on. He'd never encountered anybody just out walking. He straightened up and smiled in recognition at the tall dark man who stood in front of him.

"Hello Mike." He resisted the urge to say 'fancy seeing you here' on the basis that of late he had started to talk like his father. "Are you exploring?"

Mike nodded.

"I try to get out and go somewhere different most days. Just to get more of a feel of the area. And to escape from the house."

Jeremy knew the feeling. Getting out of the house, even if it was for only half an hour or so, made all the difference. When he was a teenager, his great-aunt had told him that she walked to the local shops every day, rain or shine, even if it was only to buy some tomatoes. At the time he had thought she was quite mad. He understood now though. Even in a home that you love, the same four walls can feel oppressive if you never see anything else. He was one of the lucky ones though, he knew that. While of late he had been bored and restless and tired of his own company, he knew that he never had to wait too long before Molly or Carlos, or both, turned up. It was only a matter of time until there was the sound of somebody else in the house, somebody to talk to. And there was always the cats. He knew that he could rely on them to listen politely when he ranted about the latest missive from on high, even if they did wash their arses while he was talking. Poor old Mike had nobody now that his wife had gone. Maybe not even a cat to wash its arse.

It wasn't, he thought, as though Mike had been given time to get used to the idea of living a life on his own. At least with illness, dreadful though it was, there was probably a part of you that could start, if not coming to terms with it, at least recognising that it was a possibility. With a sudden death like a car crash, the person was literally here one minute and gone the next. Their coat still hanging up in the hall. Their slippers under the bed. Maybe even their unwashed coffee mug still standing in the sink. All you were left with was an empty house and a lifetime's prospect of dinners for one. He couldn't begin to imagine it. A secret little selfish part of him sometimes hoped that when he and Molly got old, he would go first so that he wouldn't have to face life without her. They weren't exactly love's young dream anymore but he loved her with all his heart and he wouldn't, as his father had been wont to say about his mother, swap her for a crosscut saw. Although what a crosscut saw was he had no idea. It sounded good though.

He looked at his new friend. He looked neat and tidy, his shirt and jeans were crisp and ironed. Even his trainers looked spruce. He was obviously looking after himself, and he admired him for making himself get out and about. He wasn't sure that he could have brought himself to do the same. It would be so much easier to take the soft option and just hide behind closed doors and not face the outside world. So much easier to simply collapse in a comfortable chair with a beer and read the newspaper. Probably the most exercise he would get would be flicking the remote at the television or pulling a cork from a bottle.

One of the hardest parts, he thought, was probably not so much the going out but the coming in. That would be the tough bit. Going home to an empty house. Putting your key in the front door, knowing that nobody was going to call out a greeting or ask you how your day had been. Nobody to pour you a drink and tell you that dinner was nearly ready. Nobody even to grumble at you for leaving the lights on when you left a room. And nothing but the television, the radio, and the internet for company. He was bad enough when Molly went away for a few days to visit her sister. He generally idled away the time by drinking wine, watching re-runs of detective shows on the television and talking politics to the cats. God knew how he'd cope if he was left alone permanently.

He wondered suddenly how old Mike was. It was difficult to tell and he had never been any good at estimating people's ages. But at a rough guess he would say that he looked to be a similar age to himself, perhaps slightly older. Why wasn't he at work, he wondered. Perhaps Mike mostly worked from home, like he did. It was difficult to guess from his appearance what he did though. Could be anything. He glanced at Mike's hands. Well, probably not a manual worker.

"I thought I'd have a scout round for that police officer that Margaret told us about," Mike continued. "The one that got murdered outside the Mistletoe Hotel. Professional interest," he added, and smiled.

Jeremy raised his eyebrows. Was Mike an undertaker?

"I'm a police officer. Was a police officer," Mike said, correcting himself. "I took retirement when I was offered the chance."

Jeremy smiled to himself. Of course. With that build and that air of quiet self-assurance, what else could Mike have been?

"Must be a bit boring for you now," he said. "I bet you miss the adrenaline rush, all that racing around in squad cars and feeling collars."

Mike laughed.

"Those days have long gone. Lots of work is done by civvies now and the higher up the ranks you go, the less you do any of the hands-on stuff. It's all case management now. Especially for the big cases. Most senior officers are pretty much desk-bound. All the investigating, the questioning, the dawn raids, the exciting stuff, that's all done by the junior officers. All that stuff you see on the television, where the chief inspector or whoever arrives on the scene with his sidekick, generally treading all over the evidence in the process... well, forget it. It just doesn't happen."

"Really?" asked Jeremy.

"Really," said Mike. "During the last few years I was spending most of my days shovelling paperwork. It wasn't what I joined the force for. I was glad to get out in the end."

Jeremy nodded. It sounded a bit like teaching. The higher up the ranks you travelled, the further away from the classroom you got. In some cases that was a real loss to the pupils. In others, not so much. In fact, in some instances, there had been a distinct suspicion that, in the absence of any other way of getting rid of them, certain people were promoted out of harm's way. He sighed. Lately, he'd started to wonder if he missed being in the classroom himself. Being an Ofsted inspector was, without doubt, rewarding but somehow it didn't bring the same highs that actually teaching sometimes could. While teaching at Sir Frank Wainwright's had often been what might euphemistically be called challenging, there was no denying that there had been high points. Even though more than once on a Sunday evening he had hoped to be stricken down with a mystery, albeit temporary and non-life-threatening illness.

He thought suddenly of the school play that he'd produced. That had definitely been one of the high points. If not the highest. Against all expectation the production had been a huge success. Somebody, he couldn't remember who now, had suggested an old-fashioned music hall performance and it had been amazing how many of the kids had turned out to have such unexpected talents. Who would have thought, for instance, that Jenson could do such spectacular magic tricks? To this day he still couldn't work out how he had selected the right cards from the pack, although the fact that he was a skilled shoplifter might have helped to hone his skills. And Kayleigh, the sulky, skinny refusenik who routinely picked fights with girls bigger than herself, had the purest, sweetest voice he had ever heard. When she sang 'The Boy I Love is Up in the Gallery' in her tight-waisted dress with the big sleeves that they had borrowed from the local theatrical society and which had been altered by one of the history teachers, and with the long feathered plume sweeping down from her hat, there had been hardly a dry eye in the house.

The most amazing thing of all was that there had been no backstage punch-ups, no deliberate sabotage, and no absenteeism. All the kids had attended rehearsals, even though they were held after school, and they had all worked together. The result had been what could justly be described as a splendid performance. They had been fortunate in that there had been a particularly dry spell in relation to local news and so the local press had run a big feature on it. Parents and relatives had actually turned up to watch. Both nights had been a sell-out. 'If only,' the headmaster had remarked sadly, 'we could get half such a showing at parents' evenings.' Jeremy had resisted the opportunity to point out that, unlike parents' evenings, the parents weren't there to listen to the usual litany of truancy and bad behaviour. They were there to see their children shine, and shine they had.

He wondered what those pupils had done since leaving school. They would be in their twenties by now. He hoped that at least some of them had found success somewhere, unlike those poor children who had been found dead on the golf course. They had never been given the chance to find anything anywhere.

Jeremy felt suddenly unbearably sad. Those children's lives had been snuffed out almost before they had a chance to get started. Had they ever been in a school play? Had they whispered excitedly behind the curtains as they waited their cue to start? Had they ever stood on stage, their faces shining as they heard the applause? Now he thought about it, he couldn't even put names to them. Somehow they hadn't actually been mentioned during the discussion in class. He knew the name of the man that had been arrested and of the officer who had arrested him. He knew the name of the solicitor who had represented him. Or, rather, failed to represent him. But he couldn't put a name to even one of the children who was killed. The truth was that people were generally more interested in the murderer than the people they murdered. While infamous murderers could nearly always be named, it was rare that the names of their victims were recalled with such clarity. Who now, for instance, could recall the names of more than two or three of the Yorkshire Ripper's victims, in spite of the fact that he had killed at least thirteen?

He shook himself back to the present as Mike continued talking.

"Anyway, I enjoyed the evening class. I didn't really think that I would. I only went along for something to do."

Poor Mike, thought Jeremy. He really was lonely. He wasn't surprised. There seemed to be few opportunities for older men to make new friends, and these days a man out on his own tended to be regarded with suspicion. He'd thought twice himself before starting his regular strolls in the churchyard and park, just in case somebody got it into their head that he was up to no good. He'd even thought about getting a dog to give him a reason to be out on his own, but changed his mind when he considered the likely reaction of Aubrey and Vincent. While they had been instrumental in the rescue of Buster, a tiny golden puppy, some time ago, he didn't think that they'd take kindly to a canine taking up permanent residence with them.

When had it all got so difficult, he wondered. In the old days men used to gather in the local pub. He remembered his own father going down the road 'to see Bernard' on a Friday night, Bernard being the name of the local pub landlord. At the time, as a teenager, he had despised that pub with its pints of bitter and all its old men standing about and smoking and talking about boring stuff like car engines and cricket. He had laughed about it with his friends. It didn't even have a jukebox, just a dartboard and some boxes of dominoes. It couldn't be further from the bright new building in town, one of a chain of pubs, which attracted all the young in the area, including those under-age, and where they held twice-weekly discos. It was where he and all his friends went to drink lager and meet girls. Let the old men keep their pub, they were welcome to it. He wouldn't have been seen dead in there. Had he but known it, he had been witnessing the passing of an era.

He racked his brain to think of something positive to say to Mike.

"Do you play golf?" he said at last. "There's a good course here and the members are really friendly. I'd be happy to sign you in as a guest if you want to give it a try. Talking of golf, what did you think of that last case that Margaret told us about?"

"The golf course murders?"

Jeremy nodded.

"Interesting that nobody else ever got charged, don't you think?"

"I do," said Mike. "I looked it up when I got home. Harvey was released after eight years, so there was still every chance that the real killer could be found. But, as far as I could tell, nobody else was ever even questioned. It looked like after Harvey got out, that was it. Case closed. Well, not closed exactly. Cases are never officially closed. But I doubt that it would have been high on the list, especially if resources were stretched."

"So do you think they just quietly forgot about it?"

"I wouldn't be surprised. In theory, guidelines state that unsolved murders should be examined on a regular basis, but I suspect that in some cases the examination is pretty perfunctory. Particularly when the case is really old and therefore really cold. I suppose it's understandable really. When there's crimes happening in the here and now, a cold case isn't going to be a priority."

Jeremy scuffed at a stray piece of turf while he thought about it. It was true. Every organisation had to prioritise. In education for example, when budgets were squeezed dry, the idea of giving music lessons or taking a school trip abroad, or indeed anywhere, was laughable. Rightly or wrongly, that was how it was.

"Why do they do them then? Is it to satisfy some sort of justice?" he asked.

Mike nodded.

"Yes. It would send out entirely the wrong message if we admitted that after, say, ten or twenty years, the sheet is wiped clean. And sometimes a new sweep of the evidence means that the police get lucky. People's priorities change. Loyalties change."

Jeremy was interested.

"What do you mean?"

"Well, a wife or husband for instance, might feel compelled to stick by their spouse at the time. Twenty or thirty years down the line they might feel completely differently. Or somebody has died so they're no longer a threat, which releases people to come forward."

"I guess so. How did Harvey come to be released in the end, do you know? I mean, presumably it didn't just happen. Somebody must have done something to get the ball rolling."

"Apparently, a group calling themselves Justice Today took up the cause. They were a group of law students from somewhere up north. Anyway, one of them came across the story and it seems they decided it was just what they needed to put themselves on the map."

Jeremy smiled.

"Well, it didn't work. I've never heard of them."

"I hadn't either. Anyway, whatever they did, it succeeded. The case got referred to the Criminal Cases Review Commission who in turn recommended it for appeal. Given the lack of real evidence and the nature of Harvey's confession, my guess is that the appeal was practically rubber-stamped."

The two men turned along one of the overgrown paths and began strolling around the side of the church.

"I wonder where Harvey is now?" mused Jeremy. "I mean, what became of him when he got out of prison?"

Mike halted and stared for a moment into the distance.

"He died. Not that long ago. I Googled him and found a small piece in the press about it. It was reported because of his link to the golf course murders. He'd been living in some kind of sheltered accommodation not far from here. I shouldn't think it was much of a life."

"What did he die from?"

"Congenital heart failure, according to the newspaper."

The two men fell silent for a moment. The spectre of a weak-minded individual who had just spent a number of years in prison trying to stumble his way through life on his own was not one that really bore thinking about. Another victim of the golf course murderer.

"Do you think that once they got him to confess, the police just stopped looking for anybody else?" asked Jeremy eventually.

Mike thought for a moment.

"Pretty much. I mean, what would be the point? Waste of resources. As far as the public were concerned, the police had their man. Even if some of them suspected that they hadn't. I mean, the police themselves must have had their doubts. Margaret's point about Harvey not being able to drive was a good one."

Jeremy nodded.

"True," he agreed. "The golf course is on the edge of town. He could hardly have carried the boy's body through the streets." He thought for a moment. "But the murders did stop once he was arrested. Why was that do you think?"

Mike shrugged.

"Anybody's guess, really. Who knows? Maybe the real murderer died."

"Or moved away?" suggested Jeremy.

"I thought about that when I was looking the case up. I started searching for similar murders in other parts of the country that happened around that time, or fairly soon after."

"And were there any?"

Mike shook his head.

"None that I could find. It's a really odd case. Serial killers are called serial killers for a reason. They don't just start and then stop. They usually carry on until they're caught. So either there was some specific motive directly related to the victims, or the murderer himself was removed from the picture." Mike paused while he thought about it. "It is interesting though. I mean, it's fairly certain, because of the DNA, that Harvey was innocent of any involvement so that would indicate that the real killer is still free. But, as we've said, whoever it was didn't kill again. At least, the same DNA didn't turn up at any murder scene."

CHAPTER SIX

I t had been such a small thing. Such a silly accident to happen. Even the coroner had remarked on it. And when all was said and done, it was his own fault. He only had himself to blame. The mower was old. They'd had it for years. A great beast of a thing, it had been a state-of-the-art electric mower in its day, it had originally belonged to his father and he was oddly attached to it. When it broke down, which it frequently did, he preferred to meddle about with it rather than consider the possibility of buying a new one. Why he persisted was beyond her. It wasn't as if they couldn't afford it. But he seemed to take some kind of manly pride in tipping it up and rummaging around in its workings. And each time he got it choking back into something resembling working order, he would square his shoulders in triumph and carry on marching up and down the lawn with it.

That day, she had studied him through the open kitchen window. His hair was grey now and thinning on top, although he tried to hide it with judicious use of the comb, but he was still relatively slim and active. Retired and comfortably off, these should have been some of the happiest years of their lives. The children, Jack and Anna, had grown up and left home. They were both living independently and making their way in the world, Jack in Manchester with his partner, and Anna in New Zealand with her husband and children. As far as she and Raymond were concerned, there was nothing that they really wanted that they couldn't have. They should have been taking cruises, dining out in decent restaurants, doing things together like other couples whose children had flown the nest did. Instead, they merely drifted through the days, rarely engaging in conversation other than the most banal of exchanges. He was still active in the Masons and regularly met with his friends at the lodge. Occasionally he would invite her to join him when there was some kind of dinner dance or other event on. Just to keep up appearances. But he had never returned to the golf course. He had suddenly developed a mysterious back complaint which prevented him from playing.

She had watched him as he pulled and tugged at the mower, his shirtsleeves rolled up to the elbows, his brow furrowed as he had attempted yet again to coax the machine back into life. Her mind had run back, as it so often did, to that day she had first discovered the diary. It was a day which would be forever etched in her memory, a day in which her life had dwindled and diminished until she hardly knew herself anymore. The contented housewife that she had been had drained quietly away and been replaced by a silent, watchful wraith.

From then on, she had moved mechanically through the days, making sure that the children were fed and cared for, keeping the house fresh and clean, picking up his suits from the cleaners, arranging his dental appointments. All the tasks that she had once been happy to do became part of a dreary routine. She had thought of leaving him, of course she had. Often, and especially after the children had left home, but somehow she had always stayed and plodded on, conscious that the weeks, the months, the years of her life, were slipping past.

Before she had found the diary, if she had been asked, she would probably have said that women with abusive or unfaithful husbands should leave them. That they should just walk away if they didn't like it. They weren't living in the dark ages, women were free to make their own decisions. They didn't need a man to support them or validate their existence. It was an attitude she knew she had inherited from her mother and, until then, she had never questioned it. Warm and comfortable, secure in a happy marriage with a nice home and a decent husband, her mother had no understanding of the reality of such circumstances.

She had been looking for their passports when she found the diary. He always kept the family passports in his desk and she had an idea that they would shortly expire. Trying to pull out the bottom drawer she had found herself meeting resistance. Forcing her hand into the gap she had felt something wedged tightly against the back. She had tugged it out and found herself holding a blue leather diary that she had never seen before. It was wrong, she knew, to read other people's diaries. But surely she had a right? Raymond was her husband, he shouldn't be hiding things from her. For several moments she had stared down at it, longing to open it while trying to justify it to herself. Her heart pounding and her mouth dry, she had finally turned to the first page. Skimming through the entries, she had felt herself go cold, her mind unable to accept what she was reading. And then, just as she had thought that it couldn't get any worse, out had tumbled a number of small Polaroid photographs, the kind taken from an instant camera. The camera that she had bought for Raymond several birthdays ago. The camera with which he had taken photographs at Anna's birthday party.

She had picked the photographs up with trembling fingers

and looked at the first image. A handsome young man with thick fair hair, naked, with his back to the camera, his head coquettishly tipped over his shoulder, was winking at the photographer. A slick of vomit rose in her throat as she turned to the second. The same young man sitting on Raymond's desk, shirtless and with his thumbs hooked provocatively into the waistband of his jeans, smiled directly at her. And then the third. She had stared down at an image so alien to her that at first she hadn't been able to work out what it was. The slow realisation of what she was looking at had thudded into her consciousness and her whole married life – the life in which she had been so content and so happy, had in the space of a few minutes, completely evaporated. Stumbling backwards, her hand over her mouth, she had raced to the bathroom where she had been violently sick, retching and heaving until there was nothing left to bring up. Wiping her face with a cool flannel, she had tried to gather her thoughts. The obvious thing to do was to leave him. That had been her first thought. But it had been followed hard on its heels by a second and then a third as her heart rate slowed and the practicalities crowded in on her.

She had replaced the diary as she had found it. She needed time to think, to make a plan. She couldn't just up sticks and go. If he knew that she had seen the contents of the diary it would force a confrontation, and how would that help? Closing the study door behind her, she had unlocked the French doors and walked through into the garden. She needed fresh clean air. Untainted air. At the end of the garden was a small stone seat. They had bought it at a garden exhibition when they had first been married. Suddenly the urge to break it, to take a hammer and smash it to smithereens, to engage in an act of furious wanton destruction, flooded through her. For a moment the temptation was almost irresistible. Instead, she had walked towards it and sat down.

That evening when he had returned home she had acted as normal. Placing his dinner on the table she had asked, as always, how his day had gone. When he had said after dinner that he had some papers to sort in his study, she had simply nodded and continued stacking the dishwasher. On the surface, nothing had changed. But twice a week, when he had gone to work and the children had gone to school, she would take herself to the local library.

Scanning the local papers she would turn first to properties to rent and then to employment vacancies. With an increasing sense of frustration, she had quickly realised that the practicalities stopped her at every turn. In reality, her options were limited to the point of non-existence. Even if she had found the courage to leave, the flats and houses that she saw advertised required a hefty deposit, which she didn't have. The jobs required experience and qualifications, which, again, she didn't have. Those jobs that didn't were generally part-time and simply didn't pay enough to support herself and the children. Having attended the kind of school at which boys took apprenticeships or worked in a factory and girls worked in offices or shops, she hadn't ever had anything resembling a career. Along with many of her friends, she had left school at fifteen. Her first and only job had been in a small accounts office where her duties consisted mainly of filing, sorting the post and making tea. She had given it up, as expected, when she had the children. As a result, she was stuck. She couldn't have bound herself more tightly if she had forged the chains herself.

When she was a teenager she had once heard two women talking in the local post office, one of whom had been holding a little savings book. It was, she had confided to her friend, her running away money. At the time she had thought it was funny, a kind of joke that the women were sharing. She didn't see the funny side of it later. During her married life she had no money of her own, no means of getting any, and certainly no reserves to fall back on. He had handled all the household finances. If she had been asked how much they paid for their gas or electricity, she would have had no idea. All she had was what he called her housekeeping from which she bought the food, and her allowance for personal spending from which she bought clothes for herself and the children. Both sums were paid monthly by him into her account and she had no doubt that the payments would cease as soon as she closed the door behind her.

It was all very well people talking about rights and entitlements, but she would have to enforce them, almost certainly through the courts, which would require access to finances and could take months. In the meantime, she would still have to survive. And it wasn't as if she just had herself to think of. She had two children to consider. Her parents would have taken them in, she was sure of it, but every time she thought of walking down that familiar path and going back through that familiar front door, it was as if she was stepping into an abyss, tumbling free-fall into a dark future that held no hope.

The ignominy of returning to the council estate which she had left so proudly and so willingly would have been hard to bear. She had got used to her lovely, big, Edwardian house in the upmarket area of town that Raymond had inherited from his parents. She had grown to love its parquet flooring and beautiful mature garden, its big bay windows and light-filled rooms. She had grown accustomed to the new way of living that meant she thought nothing of changing her car every two or three years, of going food shopping without looking for the best bargains, unlike her mother who had spent all her married life doing just that. Being married to Raymond, a doctor whose father had been a doctor before him, brought with it a kind of status that she had never experienced before, a kind of lifestyle that she had only ever seen portrayed on the television. But underneath it all, deeper than the fear of losing all the trappings of the middle-class life to which she had become so easily accustomed, greater fears bubbled and seethed.

Worse than the prospect of loss of status, worse than the fear of having no money or losing her car, was the fear of her reason for leaving him somehow being exposed. For then she would not just be an object of pity, but she would be openly despised. The inhabitants of the estate where she had been born and grown up were, for the most part, decent people but some of them, she knew, resented the fact that she had escaped. Some of her old school friends thought that she had got above herself and would delight in her downfall. And apart from the effect on herself, how could she visit that on her parents? On her children? That was supposing that she even still had the children, which was the greatest fear of all. Raymond was a doctor. He was clever, he could say things about her. Things that would result in the children being taken away from her, and then what would she do?

She had tried as hard as she could to push it all to the back of her mind, fooling herself into thinking that some solution would present itself, that some way out would be shown to her. If she just sat tight, somehow all would be well. When, in spite of her best efforts, it clambered its way back to the surface, she would try to pretend to herself that she had imagined it. That she hadn't looked in his desk that day, that she hadn't found the diary. Or, if she had, then she had been mistaken. It was all something quite innocent. But then, every now and again, in the quiet of the day, when she had the house to herself, she had found herself standing behind his chair again, one hand gripping the back, her fingers itching to scratch at an old wound.

Each time her hands had trembled as she pulled out the diary, her heart fluttering as she scanned the latest entry. More than once she had steeled herself to challenge him, rehearsing what she would say over and over, willing herself to find the courage to sputter out the words she needed. The words she needed to tell him that she knew his secret, that she had seen the evidence.

Looking back, there had been an air of unreality about that period of her life. She had drifted through the days, going through the motions, getting the children ready for school, going shopping, cooking dinner. Making plans, always making plans. Their early married life had become like a forgotten story, an alternative universe which she had once inhabited. She had felt lonely and cold and often as though she was waiting for something or someone. She was, she suspected now, waiting to be rescued. Waiting for the knight in shining armour to come riding in and sweep her up, to tell her that the nightmare was over and that everything could go back to normal. In those days she thought often of Brian. Her first and only boyfriend before she met Raymond. Dear gentle Brian, content with his apprenticeship and Friday night lagers. Kind, considerate Brian, who had eventually married one of her friends and now lived in a tidy little house on the other side of town.

They hadn't invited her to the wedding. She didn't blame them. She hadn't expected to be invited and she wouldn't have been allowed to go even if she had been. Raymond had long since taken over the control of her everyday life, monitoring where she went and who she went with. Her friends, such as they were, were all wives of his colleagues. Older than her, smarter than her, none of them were the kind of women she could ever confide in. And every day he diminished her just a little more, chipping away at her self-confidence by criticising her appearance and questioning her ability to perform the simplest of tasks. Even grilling fish fingers for the children appeared to require his interference. He had heaped it on by continually dismissing any opinions that she had held, until she had ceased to have any. It was as though he blamed her for marrying him, even though he had been the one who had done the pursuing. She had become what she had once heard her mother call a friend who had been recently widowed – a shadow of her former self. That was what she had become. A shadow. It was a good description.

That summer, when those children went missing, he became even more distant. There was a subtle change in him. A watchful air, a sense of treading carefully, and he stopped dropping in at the golf club for a drink on his way home from work. Oh, he had played his part well. He had joined the neighbours in searches, scouring the local parks and playgrounds, contributing to a reward fund for any news that might lead to their recovery. He had asked her what she thought could have happened to them, one of the few occasions in recent months that he had solicited her opinion on anything. He had told her repeatedly to make sure that their own children never went anywhere unaccompanied. As if she needed telling. And all the while regarding her with that quizzical look in his eye, as if assessing exactly how stupid she really was.

And stupid she had been. She knew now that their marriage had merely been a cover. Why else would a suave, urbane professional man pluck a pretty young girl from a council estate and marry her? It wasn't as though they had anything in common. And he had reached an age where he wanted children of his own and there she was. The perfect brood mare. Innocent and malleable. Or, as she now thought of herself, stupid and gullible. At least he had provided a safe and comfortable home for their children. Happy and secure, seemingly oblivious to any strain in the family home, Jack and Anna had grown into confident successful adults. They had never had the faintest idea of there being anything the least untoward and for that, at

least, she was thankful. But what a terrible indictment it was –
that the best thing you could say about your husband was that
he did his duty by his children. It was, by any standard, setting
the bar pretty low.

She had watched him that day, fussing and tutting, as he
fiddled with the mower, his thin mouth set tight and the sweat
stains darkening against his shirt, and she had felt the buried
rage of all her wasted years, the youth that she might have
enjoyed, billow up inside her. Her eye had strayed to the socket
by the window, the mower cable trailing out of it. He'd had the
sense to switch it off at the mains. Of course he had. Without
pausing to think, she had simply switched it back on and hoped
for the best. Or the worst.

The next day, she had started leaving flowers on the
children's graves.

CHAPTER SEVEN

Aubrey looked at Vincent as he arched his sleek back and reached up to trim his claws against the bark of the tree. Aubrey manicured his own claws against one of the fence-posts in the garden, but Vincent always seemed to prefer something more wild, something more rugged. It was part of his nature, he guessed. There was something about Vincent that never seemed to take the easy route. He waited for him to finish and then strolled over to join him. Together they settled down and watched as Carlos peered down at the headstones, phone in one hand and flowers in the other. It was, they knew, Teddy who had suggested that he bring flowers. When he had told her about the murdered policeman and shown her the picture of his grave that Jeremy had taken on his phone, her pretty heart-shaped face had looked stricken.

"Oh Carlos, that poor man. How dreadful. Imagine being attacked and then just left to die on a freezing winter night."

For Aubrey and Vincent, comfortably parked on top of the chest of drawers under the window and relishing the last of the day's sunlight streaming in, it didn't take too much of a stretch of the imagination. For a cat or dog without a home, it was a stark reality. That, and being hit by a car. When Aubrey's first owner had died and he had been out on the street, the most dreadful nights had been when the winter had set in and he had felt the need to keep moving lest his paws should stick to the frozen ground. On those nights he had sought shelter where he could, no matter how insalubrious. The worst had been the public toilets near the station, where he'd accidentally found himself locked in one night. It wasn't so much the surroundings as the rank and acrid smell which had seemed to cling to his fur for days. The experience had, however, taught him a valuable lesson. Namely, always check out alternative exits.

They watched now as Carlos poked among the graves, leaning over and peering at the inscriptions, the flowers that Molly had given him permission to take from the garden looking slightly sorry for themselves as he clutched their stems. Straightening up, he sighed and stuffed the flowers in the pocket of his parka. He touched the screen of his phone.

"It's no good, Teddy. I can't find him. I mean, I know he's here somewhere, but..." He raised the phone as he spoke and waved it around him, the camera capturing the wide sweep of the churchyard. "Look. He could be anywhere."

He lowered his phone again and Teddy's face filled the screen, her voice filtering out into the spring air.

"Oh, don't give up, Carlos. We know that he's there somewhere. Didn't Jeremy say whereabouts he is?"

Carlos thought for a moment.

"He said it was over to the east." He paused. "Which way is east?"

"I don't know."

Carlos raised his head and looked about him. He sighed. It was all very well being taught in school about Amazonian rainforests and the challenges of resource management in urban environments, but he still didn't know where east was. Or west, south and north come to that. And from the sound of it, neither did Teddy and she went to a posh school. Jeremy knew though. He always knew things like that. Somehow he just did. Like he always knew where a country was without having to look it up. And he knew other stuff too, like about classical music and that. It was a mystery where he'd got all that knowledge. Perhaps it just sort of happened when you were properly grown up.

He looked back down at the screen again as Teddy continued talking.

"If we can't find it, I suppose we could just put the flowers on any grave. As a sort of token."

Carlos felt suddenly cheered. He loved it when she said 'we'. Like it was just the two of them. The rest of the world didn't get a look-in. And what she said about the flowers made sense. Cornelius Bennett was long gone. If he was in what his mother used to call 'a better place' then he'd know that they'd brought flowers for him. He wouldn't mind if they were placed on a different grave. And if he wasn't in a better place then he wouldn't know anyway.

"Good idea."

He leaned over the nearest grave and read the inscription.

"What about this one?"

"What does it say?"

"It says, '*Here lies Walter...*' something. I can't make out the last name. It's pretty old anyway."

"Good. We mustn't leave anything on a new grave because someone visiting might wonder where the flowers had come from and they might get upset. It could be a wife or husband and they might think the person in the grave had a secret lover or something and then it would ruin the rest of their life."

Carlos smiled. Teddy could weave a story out of anything.

"It's okay, the more modern graves are in a different area. Look, over there."

Holding his phone aloft he swung it round to show Teddy.

In the background, unseen by him but watched by Aubrey and Vincent, a woman knelt by three graves and placed a small posy on each.

CHAPTER EIGHT

Jeremy looked up as Carlos came into the kitchen. From his place where he had been pointedly nudging his food bowl around in the hope of attracting some attention, Aubrey silently admitted defeat and padded over to greet him. Carlos leaned over and tickled his ears before slumping down on a kitchen chair and pinning his elbows to the table. He hoped that the flowers he had placed on Walter's grave yesterday hadn't been washed away by this morning's rain, otherwise it would all have been a bit of a wasted effort. Still, it was the thought that counted. At least he and Teddy had made the effort, which was probably more than anybody else had done in the last hundred years.

Jeremy glanced up at the clock.

"What are you doing back so early? Did you have a lecture cancelled?"

"College is closed."

"Why?"

"Because of what happened. They sent us all home."

Jeremy finished the piece of toast he had been eating and took a mouthful of coffee. "Why? What happened?"

"It's that teacher."

Jeremy gave an inward sigh. Carlos had an infuriating habit of assuming other people would automatically know what he was talking about. Had he been like that as a teenager? Probably.

"What teacher?"

"That one that told you about the murders and that."

"Margaret?"

Carlos nodded.

"What about her?"

"She's in hospital."

Carlos spoke in a flat tone, his face expressionless. Jeremy sat up straighter.

"What happened? Is she ill? Has she had an accident?"

"No."

"Why is she in hospital then? And why is the college closed?"

Aubrey watched as Jeremy struggled to keep the impatience out of his voice. Aubrey knew from experience that when Carlos had something important to say, it didn't do to rush matters. It simply flustered him. He watched him as he gathered his thoughts. He looked, Aubrey thought, rather pale. He was obviously upset.

Carlos scraped back his chair and walked over to the sink. Filling a glass tumbler with water he stared for a moment out at the garden, watching the rain spatter against the window. Keeping his back to Jeremy he spoke in a low voice.

"She got attacked."

"What happened?" Jeremy repeated.

Carlos shrugged.

"I'm not sure. It happened in the college car park last night. There's police all over the place. We all had to go to the lecture theatre in groups while the principal told us about it and said that we had to say if we knew anything, and then she sent us home."

Aubrey thought for a moment about the college car park. It was surrounded by fields with a narrow path running along the back, which many of the students used as a short cut into town when they had time between classes. Some of the fencing was broken and it was easy to slip in and out. The local cats used it too, sometimes meeting up there at night for updates, like the rumour of a stray dog on the loose or reports of a missing friend. He'd been over there with Vincent only the other week when Vanessa, a small ginger cat, had disappeared. The car park was supposed to be lit at night but more often than not it wasn't. If you were going to attack somebody it was as good a place as any.

Jeremy put his coffee mug down and stared at Carlos's back.

"What did the principal tell you?"

Carlos turned to face him.

"She said that she was telling us because she didn't want people speculating." He paused. "What does that mean? Does it mean, like, making stuff up?"

"Sort of. Go on. What else did she say?"

"She said that Margaret was teaching some course last night and someone just came up to her and hit her on the back of the head when she was getting into her car to go home. With a blunt instrument. Is that, like, something heavy?" he added.

Jeremy nodded.

"Yes. Something with a bit of weight to it."

"What, like a hammer?" suggested Carlos, momentarily distracted.

"Could be." Jeremy paused. "Why on earth would anybody attack Margaret?"

"Some of the kids were saying that it was a mugging but then somebody said that nothing was taken."

Ah, thought Aubrey. Good old somebody. Same in the cat

world. Somebody always knew something. Like that time somebody had said that Jolly had once won a prize in a local cat show and they had all scoffed. Jolly, a big bruiser of a cat with a few missing teeth and a lopsided jaw that made it look like he was always smiling, was about the last feline likely to win a prize in a cat show. Or any other show, come to that. But, he reflected, on that occasion somebody had been right. Jolly had indeed won a prize in a cat show. For being the most cheerful-looking. Hence the name Jolly. He glanced across at Vincent who had just sidled round the utility-room door. He often sat in there on his own. Aubrey had asked him once what he did in there. Just thinking, Vincent had said. Just thinking.

"And somebody else said that she still had her handbag with her," continued Carlos. "So I don't think it could have been a mugging. I mean, a mugger would have just grabbed it and run. But when you think about it, whoever it was that did it must have been hanging around. I mean, like, nobody just goes walking round a car park. Especially at night."

That's all you know, thought Aubrey. He and Vincent went walking in all sorts of places, and night time was often the best time to do it. Slipping through the shadows was one of the things that they did exceptionally well. But, he reflected, they had different priorities to the likes of Jeremy and Carlos. Priorities that occasionally required the cover of darkness.

Jeremy nodded.

"True. It was probably just opportunistic. Poor Margaret. Wrong place, wrong time. What a terrible thing to happen."

He resisted the urge to add that he wondered what the world was coming to these days.

"She was found this morning," said Carlos. "Her car was parked right at the back, near the broken fencing, so nobody noticed for ages."

Jeremy looked puzzled.

"Why would she park her car at the back of the car park? Why not at the front, near the buildings?"

He had told Molly time and again to make sure that whenever possible, and especially at night, to try to park somewhere conspicuous where there were plenty of people around. It was bad enough that there were weirdos out there looking for prey, without making it easy for them.

"Probably the car park was full," said Carlos. "Not just with the evening classes. There's loads of other stuff goes on at the college. Like meetings and groups and that. And the training restaurant was all booked up as well. You have to get in really early to get a space."

Jeremy nodded. Some of the modern colleges were like great cruise ships, as he knew from inspections, with everything built on different levels and corridors that meandered in all directions. You could wander around for what seemed like hours before you found yourself in the right area. He thought for a moment about his own recent visit to the college for his evening class. When he'd set off, he'd left home in plenty of time in case he couldn't find the right room or something. And Carlos was right. The car park had been pretty full when he arrived, even though it was half an hour before evening classes were due to start.

He got up and started to clear his plate and mug from the table before suddenly realising that he hadn't asked the obvious question.

"She is still alive? I mean, she's not..."

Carlos shook his head.

"No, not the last I heard, but she was quite badly hurt. Someone said that she was barely conscious. She's in intensive care. She was found by Rubble. He passed his driving test last month."

He paused and looked thoughtful. As well he might,

thought Aubrey. He knew Rubble, Carlos had brought him home once or twice. Real name Barney, Rubble was an amiable, friendly boy who could best be categorised as one of the willing but not very able brigade. How he had managed to pass anything was a mystery to all concerned, not least Rubble himself.

"And his dad's just bought him a car," continued Carlos.

He grinned suddenly. The first time he'd smiled, thought Aubrey, since he'd come home.

"It was supposed to be for when he passed his college exams. But his dad must have realised that would be like, never, so he got it anyway. Rubble was late this morning, that's why he had to park up at the back."

Aubrey twitched his ears. He was amazed that Rubble had noticed anything. How helpful, he wondered, would Rubble be to the police?

"Rubble told us," continued Carlos, "that he couldn't work out what it was at first."

No surprise there, thought Aubrey.

"And then he realised that it was a pair of legs. Sticking out of her car. She must have been reaching over for something and then someone came up behind her and bashed her."

Carlos sat back down at the table and rested his cheek on his hand.

"It's funny when you think about it..."

"What is?"

"Well, like she goes round talking about old murders and that." He paused. "And then the next thing, she gets bashed on the head."

Jeremy felt in his pocket for his phone. When, he wondered, had he started to carry it around with him? There had been a time when mobiles were for the young, for the so-called upwardly mobile. They were something that older people jeered at. Now they were ubiquitous. He couldn't think of a single soul who didn't have one. It went everywhere with him and he would no more leave the house without it than venture out without his keys and wallet.

"I think I'll give Mike a ring," he said.

CHAPTER NINE

Aubrey settled himself on the windowsill and tucked his paws beneath him. He half-closed his eyes as he considered the tall man sitting at the kitchen table, his long legs crossed at the ankles, one hand checking his phone. He seemed all right. He had stroked Aubrey as he came in and showed no sign so far of being unfriendly. But he'd keep his distance for now. You could never tell. He still hadn't forgotten Dave, builder un-extraordinaire at their last house, who had taken any opportunity to tread on his tail or aim a passing kick at him when Jeremy and Molly weren't looking. Once, when he'd found himself locked in with him he'd been forced to take refuge on the top of a wardrobe. As Vincent had once said, most of them are all right. Until they're not. Better to err on the side of caution. Always.

"Here you go." Jeremy passed a mug to Mike before settling himself down on the chair opposite him. "So, what do you think? Do you think there's a connection?"

Mike put his phone away and cleared his throat. He looked, Aubrey thought, slightly uncomfortable. Like that time Jeremy and Carlos had to tell Molly that they'd been kicking a ball about in the garden and one of them had managed to whack it straight at her favourite terracotta pot which had tumbled over onto the path and broken. They had kept a poker face about which one of them it was, although Aubrey knew full well that it was Carlos, having seen all the action from the shed roof where he'd been sunbathing.

"I think that there's something I should tell you."

Aubrey sat up slightly straighter. This sounded interesting. Presumably Mike hadn't been kicking a ball about in their garden and breaking flower pots, so what did he have to say that gave him that furtive look?

"When I asked Margaret about any notorious crimes in the area... well, it wasn't quite the general question that everyone assumed." He tailed off and dipped his head to his mug of tea.

Jeremy stared at him.

"Wasn't it?"

"No. The thing is..." Mike hesitated for a moment and then ploughed on. "You see, the thing is, I knew the golf course victims. Well, not me personally, but my wife Rosie did. She lived on the same street as one of them. They played together when they were children. My wife was born here and she always wanted to come back. That was why we moved here when I left the police. She still has, had," he corrected himself, "family in the area."

"Right."

Jeremy, Aubrey could see, was at a loss as to what to say.

"Anyway," Mike continued, "she'd told me the story about the children going missing and how they were discovered, and the effect that it had on the community. She told me that she would usually be out playing with them but she had mumps that summer so she had to stay at home. If it hadn't been for her being ill, there might have been three dead girls instead of two. She said it haunted her for years."

He paused for a moment. Aubrey studied him. He looked older suddenly, his genial expression of moments earlier replaced by the marks of grief stamped across his face. His wife had escaped the appalling fate of her friends, only to be killed before her time in an accident. It didn't seem fair. But then, what was? Why did some cats and dogs go to kind and loving owners, while others seemed to have been picked only to be neglected and abused? The only sensible thing that an animal who found themselves in that situation should do was to leg it, but that wasn't always easy either. Lots of animals with abusive owners simply stayed put, any spirit that they once had being beaten out of them. He pushed the thought away. There was enough pain and misery in the world without him dwelling on it. He was one of the lucky ones and he knew it.

Mike cleared his throat and took another mouthful of tea as though to steady himself.

"After she died, I found myself thinking about what might really have happened that summer. I knew that the real murderer had never been caught so when we were in Margaret's class I couldn't resist asking about it. I wanted to find out more. I suppose it felt like it would give me something to do as much as anything." He gave a wry smile. "There's only so much cricket you can watch on television."

Jeremy leaned forward.

"So what have you found out?"

"Well, I started with making notes about what I already knew. Rosie had said that when the children first went missing, lots of people just thought that they were playing some sort of game and had lost track of the time. In fact, it wasn't until early evening and the children hadn't come home for their tea that anybody even thought to raise the alarm. Of course, it was a more innocent age then. Children often went off on their own. I know that I did. I expect that you did too."

Jeremy thought for a moment. It was true. He had often played out all day. One summer, when he was about ten or eleven, he and a small group of friends had bought some kind of travel card. It had enabled travel on any bus or Tube all over London. And travelled they had, spending all day hopping on and off buses and trains as the fancy took them. His parents had been quite happy about it. In fact, they had given him money to buy sandwiches and a little notebook in which to jot down anything that he had seen of particular interest. He'd still got it somewhere, along with the travel card that he'd pasted inside it. But children didn't do that now. In fact, he wouldn't be surprised if some children had never even been on a bus. And he couldn't remember the last time he had seen children playing in the street.

When he was a child the custom had been to knock on friends' doors and ask if they were coming out to play and when enough of them were gathered, they headed off to the park to play football or set up camp in the little wood nearby. Sometimes they would ride for miles on their bikes, returning only when they were hungry or the light had gone. Kids didn't do that now. Instead, they had something called play-dates, arranged for them by their parents, and when they got a bit older they sat around in each other's bedrooms or went to after-school clubs. They didn't just go off on their own, 'in case something happened'. And in the case of the golf course murders, something *had* happened. He felt suddenly sad. Sad and old. He sat quietly while Mike talked.

"Rosie said that the parents of the victims never got over it, which I guess is hardly surprising. One couple moved in the end, somewhere in the west country I think. The others stayed in the area but they got divorced." Mike paused and took a mouthful of tea. "It's not uncommon. Parents of victims often separate."

"That's odd when you think about it," said Jeremy. "You'd think that the shared grief would bring them closer together."

Mike shrugged.

"I think that it probably does to start with but then I guess that the weight of it becomes too much. It becomes the thing that binds them. I remember a case I was involved in years ago where the mother of the victim told me that it had got to the point where she couldn't bear to look at her husband anymore because all she could see was a reflection of her own grief." He paused for a moment. "One of the things I never quite understood though, is how two children were killed at the same time. I mean, as far as I know they were both strong healthy girls. One of them, surely, could have struggled free?"

"Not necessarily," said Jeremy. "The thing about children, even older children, even these days, is that they usually do what they're told. Especially if an adult with authority is doing the telling. Which, when you think about it, would have made Harvey an even more unlikely contender. He was an adult, true, but definitely not an authority figure. Children would be more likely to tell him what to do than the other way round."

Mike nodded.

"True. Rosie described him as the archetypal gentle giant. She said he was big and sort of shambling-looking, but he didn't mean any harm. None of the children were afraid of him, at any rate. They used to invite him to their birthday parties." He smiled suddenly. "She said that he used to play games with them and everybody always wanted Harvey on their team when they played rounders in the park, because he could hit the ball further and ran faster than all the kids. My wife said that some of the older children used to try to get him to buy cigarettes for them, but he wouldn't."

"Not that stupid then," said Jeremy. "Or, at least, he had a sense of right and wrong."

"I guess so. Anyway, I asked about the case in class because I was curious to know if people still remembered it."

"Do you think it's connected? To Margaret's attack, I mean?"

"Well, I think it's an odd coincidence. There she is, talking about the book that she's writing that concerns an unsolved murder and telling us that she's uncovered some new facts, and the next thing she gets hit on the head. I mean, the question has to be asked."

Jeremy nodded.

"That's what Carlos said."

Not quite, thought Aubrey. But it amounted to the same thing. Coincidences were few and far between, as he very well knew. Like that time Rupert and Roger, the Siamese that had run the manor in their previous neighbourhood, had suddenly appeared out of nowhere when some of the other cats had been planning a coup. It had been no coincidence that Rupert and Roger's nark, Lupin, had been spotted sneaking away from the meeting and hot-pawing it off in the direction of their garden, even though when questioned later he said that he'd just been stretching his legs.

"Do you think that the attacker intended to kill her?" Jeremy asked.

"I should think so. I mean, a blow to the back of the head with a heavy instrument is going to cause serious harm at the very least. It's not the kind of thing that you'd do by accident."

"Why do you think that the attacker didn't, well, finish her off?"

"Perhaps he thought he had. Or perhaps he lost his nerve after the first blow and just ran away."

"It might not be connected to the book she's writing though," said Jeremy. "There might well be another motive. In your experience, what are the main reasons that a person kills?"

"Greed," said Mike, thinking it over. "Anything that involves money. Power, revenge. Jealousy or fear. Anger, sometimes. And, more rarely, the good old psycho. The character who does it for enjoyment, and because they can."

Aubrey considered for a moment. He knew what a pyscho was. The man who had murdered Carlos's mother was a pyscho. So was Rupert. Not Roger though. Roger operated on cold logic. Everything he did, he did for a reason, chilling though that reason might be. He shivered slightly. He often felt cold when he thought about Rupert and Roger.

"It would help if we knew something about her," said Jeremy. "That might give us some kind of clue." He felt suddenly slightly foolish, aware that he was talking like the amateur detective beloved of crime fiction. But, he reminded himself, Mike wasn't an amateur. He'd been a police officer, and a senior one at that. So that was all right.

"We only met her once," he continued. "We don't know, for instance, if she lived alone or if she had a partner. Did you notice if she was wearing a wedding ring?"

Mike shook his head.

"Can't say I did. But that doesn't mean anything anyway. She might be living with somebody and not married to them. Or she might be widowed."

He glanced instinctively down at his own wedding ring as he spoke.

Jeremy pretended not to notice and took a mouthful of tea while he thought about it. He should, he knew, have been working on a report but this was much more interesting. In fact, if he was honest, he was sort of enjoying it. Not that he would have wished injury on Margaret, far from it, but given that it had happened, well, they couldn't do any harm. And between them they might even help to find the attacker. At the very least it would give Mike something to think about other than his dead wife.

"She might have had enemies," he said. "Or there might have been something from her past. She had been a journalist, remember. She might easily have upset somebody in the course of her work."

"True," said Mike. "But she's been retired for some time. Why wait this long if it was some kind of revenge attack?"

Jeremy thought for a moment.

"Maybe he's been in prison. Maybe she helped to put him there and he swore vengeance when he got released."

Even as he said it, he realised it sounded like something from a bad film script.

"I mean," he added lamely, "people do bear grudges."

Too right they do, thought Aubrey. That bloke whose newly laid front path he and Vincent had accidentally ruined by walking across it before it was set, still threw stones if he caught sight of them. It wasn't like they'd meant to do it. If they had, they would have got a few of the lads round to join in.

"To be honest, it's not usually journalists that are the subject of revenge attacks," said Mike. "It's more likely to be a witness at the trial that's under threat, or a member of the jury. I'm not saying that you're wrong, but let's put that idea to one side for a moment and think about the partner option. If she was attacked by a partner, why do it in a car park? Why not do it at home? To be brutal, you'd be in private, no chance of anybody seeing you."

"Spur of the moment?" suggested Jeremy. "Her husband, or whoever, thought that she was having an affair or something and followed her?"

"Possibly." Mike considered it for a moment. "But as far as we know, she was going to the college to teach, not to meet someone. Her partner, if he exists, could easily verify that simply by ringing the college and pretending he wanted to join the class or something. Unless," he conceded, "he thought that she was meeting someone afterwards. But, again, why attack her in the car park? Although it happened after dark, it's still a big open space with people coming and going. Why not just wait until she got home? In my experience, even psychos have some sense of self-preservation."

Jeremy sipped at his tea while he thought about it. Mike was right. Victims of that kind of assault were usually attacked in out of the way, lonely, places. A recreation ground at night with no dog walkers or strollers to witness anything, or a deserted building. Not a car park. Not unless it was one of those huge multi-storey ones with the echoey back stairs reeking of damp and urine and dodgy lifts. If ever there was a building designed for bad things to happen in, the multi-storey car park was surely it. But this hadn't been that type of car park.

"Maybe the attacker didn't plan it, maybe he just lost control or something," he suggested.

"Possibly," said Mike. "But whoever it was must have had a weapon to hand. If she was barely conscious when she was found, then it must have been something heavy. Not the kind of thing that you'd just happen to have in your pocket. Also, generally, attacks like these usually have some kind of inciting trigger, like being caught in the act so to speak. Or, one of the most common ones, telling him that she's leaving. That's always a dangerous flashpoint for women. But as far as we know, Margaret had taught her class and was just getting ready to go home."

"True," Jeremy conceded. "So if the motive wasn't revenge or a what do you call it, crime of passion, what do you think it could be?"

"I don't know," said Mike. "It could just be a random attack, but a crime of that nature is much rarer than you might think, in spite of what the media would have us believe. Most of our streets are safe to walk, even now." He frowned. "But, having said that, this case really does seem to be random. Nothing was stolen, and there doesn't appear to be a sexual motive of any kind..."

"Well, I only know what Carlos has told me," said Jeremy. "And he only knows what they were saying in college. I mean, it's not official or anything."

Mike thought for a moment.

"The local plods have got a social club which retired officers can join. I saw it on Facebook. Funnily enough, they meet at the golf club. I've been thinking about joining. I could take a stroll over there and see what I can find out."

"Good idea. Do you think they'll tell you anything?"

Mike nodded.

"I should think so. Once a copper... Well, it's a gang that you never really leave, even when you retire."

"Great. Definitely worth a try. But going back to motive." Jeremy paused while he thought about it. "Is it possible, do you think, that maybe it *was* intended as a robbery and whoever it was got disturbed and ran away?"

"It's possible," admitted Mike. "But if he, or she, had been disturbed, that presupposes that there was somebody else in the vicinity and sufficiently close to alarm the attacker. So why then hasn't any witness come forward and why wasn't Margaret found until this morning?"

"Good question," said Jeremy. "I mean, if it was a robbery, then why not just grab her handbag before running off? Also, she's in intensive care. It must have been a pretty savage attack. Muggers don't usually go in for that level of violence. Do they?" he added.

"Not usually," said Mike. "The general modus is to scare the victim into handing over the goods. That's why robbery is classed as a theft with the use or threat of force. Quite often there's no physical contact at all."

"I see what you mean." Jeremy spoke slowly. "If the motive was robbery, all the attacker had to do was cover his or her face and scare Margaret into handing over her bag. Why then was she attacked in such a brutal manner?"

"Barring the psycho option, the only thing that makes any sense brings us back round to the possibility that there's some connection to the book she's writing. Specifically to the new lead she thinks she's found," said Mike.

Jeremy nodded.

"It seems the most likely."

"Which brings us to the obvious conclusion that somebody didn't want that new lead found."

Jeremy stared at him.

"But that means..."

"That it's not beyond the bounds of possibility that whoever attacked her was in our class that night."

CHAPTER TEN

Jeremy turned the thought over. It would be too easy to jump to the wrong conclusion. There were other possibilities. And they couldn't entirely rule out a random attack, however rare such attacks might be. There were some very strange people out there. But his instinct told him that Mike was probably right. One of their classmates might have a very good reason for attacking Margaret. Somebody with a vested interest in keeping the case cold. Someone who knew more than they reasonably should have done about the golf course murders.

He thought about his fellow classmates. To all intents and purposes they appeared to be just ordinary people, following a nice ordinary interest. They were the sort of people that had a roast dinner on Sundays, frequently mislaid their car keys, and paid their bills on time. People like him. None of them seemed the kind to go around inflicting grievous bodily harm. But then how could you tell? Presumably Jack the Ripper had looked like everybody else. In fact, now he thought about it, looking ordinary and acting like everybody else was, surely, a prerequisite for a killer. At least, for a killer that didn't want to be caught. They didn't go about with blood dripping off their hands and foaming at the mouth and neither did they howl at the moon. At least not publicly. They were the man or woman next door. The bloke that serviced your car. The woman that served you in the post office. They were frightening in their ordinariness.

He thought about some of the notorious killers of the last hundred years. He wasn't a great studier of criminology but some names were etched on the public consciousness, probably for all time.

The case of John Reginald Christie, he of 10 Rillington Place fame, was a good example. Baggy-eyed, balding, and mild-mannered, he had been ordinary to the point of facelessness. Nevertheless, he had killed a number of women and hidden their bodies under the floorboards and in the garden. Some of them he had put in a kitchen alcove and covered it with wallpaper. And to add to the heinous nature of his crimes he had allowed a poor, intellectually weak young man to take the blame. Which in those days meant hanging. And more recently there had been the case of Dennis Nilson. A more ordinary-looking man in the street you couldn't hope to find. There was absolutely nothing remarkable about him at all. Employed at a job centre, outwardly just like everybody else, and yet he had killed men and stored and then disposed of their bodies, not just in one flat that he had lived in, but two. His crimes were only discovered when the drains appeared to be blocked.

So why not one of their classmates? Why not one of those harmless-looking women with their capacious handbags and neat little notebooks? Why not the other man with the greying hair and sensible shoes? Who knew what murderous thoughts boiled and broiled beneath the respectable exteriors? He had once heard somebody say that the banality of evil was truly chilling. He was inclined to agree.

"She might have told other people about this new lead. I mean, apart from people in our class," he said at last. "She might have talked about her book to friends and so on. As a former journalist, she's bound to have lots of connections. Maybe she did an interview about it or something."

"She might," agreed Mike. "But it's an odd coincidence that she tells all of us about it and the very next night, she gets attacked. At the college," he added.

Aubrey watched as Jeremy thought about what Mike had just said. For the first time in weeks Jeremy looked engaged and interested. He didn't know this Margaret woman they were talking about, and he wouldn't have wished any harm on her, but it was good to see Jeremy starting to look more like his old self again. Apart from anything else, he might start remembering where the cat treats were kept.

"Okay, let's have a think about it. Who was in the class that night?" Jeremy asked.

Mike sat back and thought for a moment.

"Well, us obviously. And those women who know each other. And there was another man besides us. Quiet bloke, a bit reserved. I don't think he said anything all evening, apart from to give his name. Which I can't remember," he added.

On that basis, thought Aubrey, he was obviously the attacker. He'd heard Molly say once that the quiet ones were always the worst because you could never tell what they were planning. She'd been talking about the residents at the care home where she worked, some of whom were inclined to be decidedly mischievous. But it applied to cats as well. Rafferty, the cat who lived up the road, barely said a word but it had been him who had presented them with the plan of a daring raid on the food bank. He'd noticed one night that a small window had been left open and had gone in to explore. And discovered that the food bank not only gave out food to humans but for their pets as well. Food in small foil pouches which could be opened with the judicious use of a claw and which they had carried, laboriously and working as a team, to various hiding places. It had taken them most of the night but by the time they'd finished they'd managed to take the whole lot. The local paper had been full of the mystery of the stolen pet food, with the result that some local residents who owned more than one cat or dog found themselves on the wrong side of police questioning.

"Was there anybody else there apart from the women and that man?" asked Jeremy. "We did all introduce ourselves although I can't remember most of the names. I'm trying to picture in my mind who was sitting where. Hold on a minute."

He got up and rummaged around in a drawer.

"There are still some things that smartphones don't do better."

He sat back down and flicked opened the pad at a fresh sheet. Fumbling in his pocket, he pulled out a pen. Old habits die hard, he thought. As a teacher he had always had spare pens about his person, for the inevitable pupils who turned up for lessons and appeared not to have grasped the fact that they might be called upon to participate in some way, such as writing something down.

"As far as I recall, the desks were arranged in a horseshoe shape." He drew the shape as he was talking. "And I was sitting here." He added his initials. "Where were you, Mike?"

"There," said Mike, jabbing his forefinger down on the page. "And the women, they were sort of bunched in the middle. I think that one of them was called Helen. And another one was called Diana. But I can't remember the name of the last one."

"Nor me," Jeremy admitted. He jotted the names that Mike had suggested down on the pad.

"Then there was that other bloke but I can't remember his name either."

"Okay. If we accept that it wasn't either of us..." He thought for a moment. He wasn't quite sure where he was going with this. He looked down at the notepad again and tapped the end of his pen against it.

"How likely is it do you think that the attacker was a woman?"

"It's as likely to be a woman as it is to be a man. It's not hard to swing a weight at somebody, especially if they've got their back to you."

"But a woman..." Jeremy trailed off. He had, he knew, a tendency to think of women as the gentler sex. Not given to acts of violence or cruelty. But, he reflected, how gentle somebody might be would probably depend on how much they had to lose. And in this instance, it might be quite a lot.

Mike smiled.

"One of the most violent prisoners that I ever took into custody was a woman."

Jeremy opened his mouth to ask what she'd done and then closed it again. He had a vivid imagination and there were some things that it was probably better not to know.

"What do you think would be the motive? I mean, what motive would a woman have for suppressing new facts about an old murder?"

"Well, I don't think that she was the perpetrator although I might be wrong there," said Mike. "The police, at the time, seemed convinced that a man was responsible but I'm not sure that there was any hard evidence to support that."

"What about the boy? Why do you think he was killed later?"

"I suspect that the boy was killed because he knew something. Which makes me think," he added, "that the girls knew their killer and told the boy something about him. Either that or he saw something. Remember, he was found a little time after the two girls. A little time in which he might have taken the opportunity to cause some trouble."

Jeremy fiddled with his pen while he thought about it.

"It would be helpful to know how many, if any, of the people in the class that night were living in the area at the time of the murders. And at this stage we don't even know their names for sure."

He put his pen down as the back door opened and Carlos came in, followed by Rubble.

"Carlos," Jeremy gestured towards Mike, "this is Mike. Mike, this is Carlos. And Rubble."

Carlos nodded at Mike and dipped his hand into the cat-treat tin. Hooray, thought Aubrey. At least somebody in this house still knew how to get his priorities right.

"We were just talking about what happened to Margaret at the college," Jeremy continued. "Mike used to be a senior police officer."

Carlos looked at Mike with renewed respect. He was, Aubrey could see, impressed.

"What do you think happened? I mean, do you think it was, like, some random mad person?" he asked.

Mike suppressed a smile.

"Possibly. Although in many cases like Margaret's people are often attacked by somebody that they know." He turned to Rubble.

"Are you the boy who found her?"

Rubble nodded and looked nervous. He was, Aubrey could see, trying to think of a way to deny it.

"Can you describe to me what you actually saw?"

Rubble looked at Carlos and then back again at Mike.

"Well, it was like I told the others. She was just in her car." He thought for a moment. "Sort of sticking out of it."

"With her back to you?"

Rubble nodded again, clearly unable to add anything further.

Years of teaching had taught Jeremy when to stop flogging a dead horse. He leaned back in his chair and turned to Mike.

"If only we could think of some way to get the names of the other people that attended the evening class."

"Oh, I can get those for you. My auntie works at the college," said Rubble. "I know her password."

Jeremy and Mike stared at him.

"We wouldn't want you to get into any trouble," said Jeremy.

"It's all right. She's leaving soon anyway. She's found another job."

"Is that allowed? I mean, like, is it illegal?" asked Carlos.

Rubble turned to him.

"What, getting another job?"

"No," said Carlos patiently. "Getting stuff off of computers and that."

"I suppose so. Technically," said Jeremy. "But, we've already been told the names of everyone in the class, we had to introduce ourselves, so it's not like it's anything that we don't already know. It's just that we can't remember them. So we wouldn't really be doing anything wrong. Not really."

He was, Aubrey could see, trying to salve his conscience. His face had that sort of half-smiley apologetic look, like when he tried to load Aubrey and Vincent into their cat baskets ready for the vet's annual injections. If only he knew. They could spot it coming a mile off and usually took evasive action. The last time they'd felt sorry for him and, after a short meeting to discuss the matter, had voluntarily climbed into the baskets. As

Vincent had said, it was only fair to meet him halfway now and again.

Mike looked at Rubble, curious.

"How is it that you know her password?"

"She always uses the same one. She told me."

"What is it?" asked Jeremy.

"Rubble," said Rubble.

CHAPTER ELEVEN

The three women settled themselves at their favourite table in the corner. They had long since given up going out for meals in the evening on the basis that it was too much hassle. Buses were unreliable at that time and taxis didn't always turn up, even when they'd been booked. Given that they all liked a glass or two of wine with their food, driving wasn't an option. They had settled instead into their comfortable routine of weekly lunch in the cosy little bistro in the centre of town. It was reasonably priced. They could always get a table, provided that they came midweek. And the food was good.

Having finally given their orders to the waitress the women sat back and smiled at each other. They were fortunate to have met and they knew it. All three of them widowed, all living alone, and all seeking more than the television or radio for company, they had met at an Art for Beginners class and bonded over their lack of talent. Diana, Helen and Moira, each had once been married to a professional man. As was the case so often for women of their time, theirs had always been the supporting rather than the main role. Wives to doctor, dentist, and solicitor, they had been, as one of them had once said, a modern update of Happy Families. Except that one of them hadn't been happy. One of them hadn't been happy at all.

She fished her phone from her handbag and pretended to check it while she half-listened to her friends talking as they waited for their orders to arrive. Thank God for mobiles. What did people do for distraction activities before they were invented? She couldn't remember, it was such a lifetime ago. She kept her eyes on the screen as she scrolled through. She didn't feel like joining in, but it was important that she had come today. Important that she go through the customary motions of placing her jacket on the coat stand, taking her usual seat nearest to the window and then glancing over the menu. She had been tempted to make an excuse and cry off earlier but had thought better of it. She would have to venture out at some point and it was better to get it over with now. The point was to appear normal, as though nothing had happened. At least they didn't seem to have heard the news about Margaret yet, for which she was profoundly grateful, although it would only be a matter of time. The crime rate was low in the area so that even minor criminal damage got reported. A full-blown attack on a woman in a car park was certain to make headline news in the local paper.

She felt the beginning of a nagging pain in her head. She had barely slept last night although she had stayed up way beyond her usual bedtime. Foregoing the nightly routine of brushing her teeth and moisturising her face, she had headed straight for her bedroom, and undressed quickly in the dark. She had been afraid to switch the light on for fear of what it might bring in. Afraid that she might catch sight of herself in her dressing-table mirror and see her true self reflected back at her.

She had climbed into bed and lain on her back, staring out into the darkness. When she was a child, she had been afraid of the dark, convinced that the absence of light brought all kinds of horrors with it. As an adult she had come to realise that sometimes it was good. Sometimes it was reassuring to be swallowed by the black of the night. A comfort to just freefall into the darkness.

She had lain there for several hours with eyes wide open before finally drifting off, only to be woken as dawn was breaking by Clara jumping on the bed. She had reached out and stroked her warm little head and there had been a couple of blissful moments when she had simply lain there peacefully and thought about today's meeting at the bistro and what she might wear. And then the recollection of what she had done flooded through her like iced water.

Pushing the thoughts away, she glanced out of the bistro window. Across the road, on the other side of the high street, a small group of children jostled and pushed each other at the bus stop while being reprimanded by the accompanying adults. She wondered why they weren't at school and then realised that it must be half-term. She didn't keep up with these things now her own children were grown up.

She watched them for a moment, glad of the distraction. How old were they, she wondered. Ten? Eleven? The same age as... she closed her eyes. The unbidden memories, disturbed in the silt of her consciousness since Margaret's evening class, now began their slow, eddying drift upwards again. The faces of those children as they had appeared almost every day in every newspaper danced before her eyes. The two girls, one dark and one fair. Best friends, the newspapers had said. Inseparable. Even, as it turned out, in death. And then there was the boy. Small for his age, big bright eyes and crooked teeth, head tipped to one side, he had looked as though he was just about to tell the best joke ever. The children, all three of them, had looked so happy in their photographs. None of the upsets and worries that arrive with adulthood had yet to befall them, and now they never would. They had been so trusting. So innocent. Just as she had once been.

She would give anything, anything at all, for her path never to have crossed his. If only her car hadn't broken down that day. If only it hadn't been raining. If only somebody else had stopped to help. If only... Surely two of the saddest words in the English language. That day she would have simply driven home, happy to be aged seventeen and driving her brother's car. She would have been blithely unaware of how narrowly she had averted disaster. They could have passed on the road and she would have been none the wiser as to his existence. She would, she knew with the benefit of mature years, have married Brian and stayed happily contented with him. She would have lived the life that had been more or less mapped out for her, which, until that point, had been all that she had wanted. But fate had determined otherwise and the older, suave man who had tapped at her car window, a look of concern on his handsome face, had cast the darkest of shadows over the rest of her life.

She had sometimes heard the question asked, 'What advice would you give to your younger self?' She knew what her advice would be. Don't go out driving that day. Stay at home. Close the curtains. Something wicked this way comes. But she hadn't stayed at home. She had innocently driven into a nightmare. Responding to his tapping on the car window, she had wound it down and smiled up at him. In her world, men cared for you and looked after you. They gave you help when you needed it, and here was one apparently ready to do just that. She had climbed into his car gratefully and listened as he chatted away, his strong, clean hands resting lightly on the steering wheel, the faintly disturbing scent of his cologne drifting across her senses, and she had felt herself relax. She was in the safe hands of a grown-up.

A child from a council estate, she had, through

circumstance of birth, few prospects up until that point. Although she hadn't known it, the invisible bonds of class had clutched her as tightly as a straightjacket. Fortunate enough to have been born into the welfare state she had wanted for little in material terms but culturally she was limited to what she saw around her. And what she saw around her was the life that her parents led. A life in which meals out were for occasions, the theatre was for posh people, and holidays were saved for and taken annually. Usually in the same place.

But he had changed all that. He had opened doors to places that she hadn't known were there. She had learned that not all food had to be fried or boiled and olive oil had other uses than for earache.

He was like nobody else she had ever known and in a very short space of time, she had been completely besotted with him. He had been the polar opposite to the boys of her own age who played football for local teams on Sunday mornings and only ever owned one suit, which was the one they got married in. He played tennis and cricket and owned enough suits to fill a wardrobe. Up until that point, her experience of restaurants had been confined to the relative sophistication of the Berni Inn, where wine was either white or red and the steaks were well done and always served with chips or a jacket potato with a small portion of salad on the side which nobody ate.

Suddenly it had all changed and she had found herself in small intimate places where he knew the owners by name and ordered wine without looking at the wine list. He didn't glue himself to the radio on Sundays to listen to the top twenty. He listened to classical music by composers that she had never heard of. And he had been divorced. In her world people didn't get divorced. They didn't even separate. If they were unhappy, they slugged it out until the bitter end. Sometimes literally.

Looking back, those early days seemed like a dream.

Counting the hours until he picked her up in his shiny new sports car, she had lived for their next date. She had stopped seeing her old friends. They seemed immature now, childish, with their pop posters on their bedroom walls and their Saturday morning trips to the make-up counter in Boots. And she had stopped answering Brian's calls. Poor Brian, with his big raw mechanic's hands and greasy overalls, his shy smile and gentle self-effacing manner. He hadn't stood a chance.

CHAPTER TWELVE

S itting hunched over the kitchen table, slightly overfull from the lunch with her friends, she stirred her coffee, trailing her spoon across the top and watching the tiny ripples form in its wake. The chatter of the radio lapped around her, a soothing background to the tsunami of anxiety and fear that had been threatening to erupt since she had arrived home. It had been bad enough in the bistro, all the dark memories emerging yet again, flying around her head like leaping salmon, but she had managed to suppress them. She had turned away from the window and stopped watching the children. She had immersed herself in the chatter and gossip of the group, even managing to join in and laugh at the right moments. To all intents and purposes she had been her usual self. It was different now that she was on her own.

She dropped the spoon onto the table and laced her fingers around the coffee mug, taking comfort from its gentle warmth. Outside, the rain continued, a thin spatter that had been unremitting since the morning. She stared at it for a moment, watching it beat steadily against the glass. If only she hadn't gone out last night. If only she had sat quietly at home with

Clara and watched the television or read a book. If only she hadn't yielded to the impulsive desire to take some action. To do something. Anything. All day, the fear and dread had been billowing up until the pressure had become almost unbearable. She must, she knew, protect Jack and Anna. What would the cost to them be if the truth came out? It would be bad enough for her, but she was getting old. She might even somehow weather the storm. It would be Jack and Anna that would really pay the price. Especially Jack. Always the more sensitive of the two, he would never come to terms with the truth about the father that he had admired so much. To Jack, his father had been everything that a man should be.

She had tried to suppress Margaret's words but they had filled her mind, repeating over and over, the words thundering up and crashing through her brain. Old case. New lead. Shocking exposé. Like gigantic news headlines, they had unfurled and danced before her. In her imagination Margaret's face had grown larger and larger, until it had appeared grinning and triumphant as she prepared to reveal to the world what she knew.

By evening, the urge to get out of the house had been overwhelming and she had driven, instinctively, to the college. What she thought she was going to do when she got there, she didn't know. She had parked up at the back and sat fidgeting, the images darting in and out of her head like electrical impulses. She had tried to calm herself, breathing slowly and attempting to arrange her thoughts in some kind of rational order.

What if Margaret was following the wrong scent? What if she had picked up something that was nothing to do with Raymond at all? It was entirely possible. After all, at the time the police had arrested the wrong man, so why shouldn't Margaret have gone off on a different tack as well? She was probably barking up completely the wrong tree. For several seconds she had almost managed to convince herself that must be the case, but then the serpent had slithered back in. What if, on the other hand, Margaret had somehow, against all the odds and after all these years, uncovered some new evidence? What if she really had uncovered the truth? If that was the case it would not so much blow her and her children's lives apart as smash them to smithereens.

She had dropped her forehead into her hands, pushing her palms hard against the skin as though she could force out some kind of solution. Raising her head again she had opened the window slightly, welcoming the sudden rush of cool air. She needed to think. And to think rationally. What was it that Margaret could possibly know? Surely there was nothing, especially after all this time. How could there be? There had been no witnesses. If there had been, they would have come forward at the time. Some new evidence perhaps? But what? What could have emerged now that wasn't known then?

There was the discovery of DNA, of course, and she knew that it had finally cleared Harvey of any involvement. It had made headlines in the local paper which had carried the full story. But Raymond had been cremated and she had long since got rid of any of his possessions. The only thing that she hadn't cleared was his desk, but nobody except her had been anywhere near it since Raymond had died. As far as she was aware, Raymond had never been under suspicion. But whatever it was that Margaret knew, or thought she knew, she had seemed horribly certain about it.

Tiny prickles of sweat had started to bubble along her hairline. Could she appeal to Margaret? Throw herself on her mercy? Tell her that it would ruin not only her own life but that of her children? Tell her that it would finish her, that she was too old to start somewhere new? She could point out that the story was decades old, that nobody was interested anymore. What purpose could possibly be served by resurrecting it now? Even as the thoughts formed, they shivered and dissolved.

It wouldn't work. She was fooling herself. The fact was that people were very definitely interested in historic crimes; probably even more so now than ever before, as the plethora of podcasts and documentary television programmes proved. And what was more fascinating than an unsolved crime? You only had to consider the enduring interest in Jack the Ripper to know that. There were books being written about him even now, over a century later. Besides which, Margaret was a former journalist on a national newspaper. You didn't get to be in a position like that by being soft-hearted. If she had a story then she would stick with it.

There was no getting away from it, that damned woman was going to tear her up by her roots and fling her aside. Gone would be her life as she knew it, that carefully constructed edifice that she had built up over the years would collapse in on itself as neatly as a house of cards. There would be no more cheery greetings from local shopkeepers. No more cosy lunches at the bistro. No more coffee mornings at her friends' houses. And her other activities would dry up as well. She'd probably find herself left off the volunteers roster at the food bank and her feel-good charity fundraising work would almost certainly disappear too. For what charity would want funds raised by her? It would be tainted money. She would be met with hostility and suspicion wherever she went.

She didn't kid herself that her friends would stick by her either, of course they wouldn't. Oh, they might pretend to. To begin with. But it would only be a matter of time before they started distancing themselves from her and asking each other whether she had known. It would only be a short step from there to deciding that she *must* have known. After all, she had been married to him. How could she not have known? After a while they would start avoiding her, making excuses, arranging to meet without her. They wouldn't want to be seen with her and she wouldn't blame them. Who would want to be associated with the widow of a child murderer? But all that aside, there was, as always, Jack and Anna. If it was just her then perhaps she could find a way to live with it. But Jack and Anna had been the only good things that had come out of her marriage and she couldn't, wouldn't, let their lives be ruined as hers had been.

And then she had seen her. Glancing up into her rear-view mirror, she saw the small figure crossing the car park, a large bag slung across her shoulder. She was coming towards her. Her car must be parked nearby. Without stopping to think, she had opened the car door and walked round to the boot. Pretending to rummage about inside, she opened the box that she kept meaning to take to a charity shop. She had been clearing the garage and, among other things, had discovered Jack's old dumbbells. He was clearly never going to take them away, in spite of her regular reminders, so she had lifted them into the plastic box that she had filled with unwanted items. She looked at them now and then back up at the figure, watching as she approached a small blue Citroën. Suddenly, all the rage and all the fear of years flared up inside her. Reaching forward she grasped the heaviest dumbbell and felt her shoulder sag under its weight.

CHAPTER THIRTEEN

She had driven home on automatic pilot, her brain in a fog, barely noticing the familiar landmarks. Dashing through to the kitchen, she had filled the sink with boiling water and bleach and dropped the dumbbell in. She had watched as the water closed around it. The sooner she got it off to a charity shop the better. It wouldn't matter if nobody bought it. If it sat on a shelf and gathered dust for fifty years it still wouldn't matter. The point was that it would be out of her house and would be handled by other people. She wouldn't even need to take it in personally. She could just leave it in a box in a charity shop doorway, tucked in among other items that couldn't be traced back to her. And she would make sure that she wore gloves. She'd watched enough crime drama on the television to understand the basics of avoiding detection.

Standing back, she had leaned against the wall and then slowly slid down towards the floor. Padding across the kitchen, Clara had huddled in next to her, pushing her little furry body against hers in a show of support. Squeezing her eyes shut she had stroked Clara's back and listened to her rusty little purr as she tried to gather her thoughts into some sort of order, to find some kind of justification for the dreadful act she had committed. Because she hadn't meant to do it. She hadn't planned it. Somehow it had just happened. She knew how pathetic that sounded. It would hardly stand up as a defence in court. But it was true.

When she had watched Margaret walking across the car park, apparently without a care in the world, the bitter unfairness of it all had almost taken the breath from her body. She was the one who had lived with it all these years. She was the one who had suffered in silence. Now she was going to be made to suffer again and her children would suffer even more. And then it had been as though her body had moved of its own volition and she had simply observed it. Where that uncontrollable urge for violence had come from, she had no idea. She had never been violent in her life. Even when the children were small and playing up until she had felt at the absolute end of her tether, she had never smacked them. Not once. Not even a light tap on the back of the leg. It had never occurred to her.

And now she had attacked someone. Actually physically attacked someone. With a weapon. A small groan escaped her. Had she killed her? She had hit her hard, she knew that. She had felt the sickening thump as she crashed the dumbbell down on Margaret's unsuspecting head. She had instinctively raised her arm to strike another blow and then she had frozen. She had lowered her arm in what felt like slow motion and stared at what she had done, appalled at the sight of Margaret's inert body slumped forward, one hand stretched out as though to reach for something.

Slowly, she had stepped back into reality. And then she had fled. She hadn't waited to see if Margaret was still breathing. She had simply run to her car, dumbbell still in hand, fired up the engine and made straight for home.

She stood up and poured her now cold coffee down the sink. The unfairness of it all washed over her again. She wasn't the one who had killed those children. She wasn't the one who had taken their lives. But she and Jack and Anna were the ones who were now going to pay the price. Maybe literally. If the case against Raymond was proved she might lose his pension and then where would she be? She had no pension of her own. She would have to rely on the state. She suppressed the flickers of panic that began shooting through her again. Surely they wouldn't take away a widow's pension? She pressed her lips together in an effort to remain calm. Probably not. But she would be shunned by the community, of that she was sure. She would have to not only move house but move county, maybe even move country. For how could she stand the staring and the whispering behind hands, or worse, not even behind hands. Not even whispering. But that would be nothing compared to the damage suffered by Jack and Anna. They would have the rest of their lives to live with it. They would be damned by association. By comparison with what was coming to them, Raymond had got off lightly. He had never had to face what he'd done. For the first time she regretted that he was no longer here. By her actions that summer day she had, unwittingly, given him the easy way out. Now, if the truth really was going to see the light of day, she wished with all her being that he was still alive. That she could witness him being dragged kicking and screaming from the house and thrown into prison where he could rot until he died.

She rinsed her mug and stood it on the draining board. She felt slightly steadier now. None of her friends at the bistro had said anything about Margaret, so clearly it wasn't yet common knowledge. Whatever else happened, all she had to do was remain calm. She must make herself go about her ordinary everyday business and appear as shocked as everybody else when the news about the attack on Margaret broke. Because, surely, no one would suspect her. Why would they? There was nothing to connect her with it. She was just another faceless elderly lady. There were thousands like her and most people would find it hard to tell one from another. Her stomach suddenly lurched as an appalling thought struck her. What if somebody had seen her? Had there been anybody around? She didn't think so, but she wasn't sure. It was dark and quiet at that end of the car park. But what if there were security cameras? It would be the natural place to position them. She didn't think that she'd noticed any, but then she hadn't been looking.

Walking through to the sitting room, she switched on her laptop and searched for the college. If there were any images on the college website, and surely there would be, she might be able to get a view of the car park. Locating the site, she stared at the images, running the cursor back and forth, zooming in to try to get a better look. Sure enough, the car park showed behind the main teaching block but it was impossible to see any detail. She peered more closely at the screen. There was something just to the left that might be a camera but it was difficult to tell. She sat back and closed her eyes. She had done two terrible things, but if it were not for Raymond's crimes none of it would have happened. Evil begets evil.

CHAPTER FOURTEEN

Jeremy, Carlos and Aubrey sauntered along the overgrown path. The rain had washed the ground and the air smelt fresh and clean. Carlos was glad that he'd decided to join Jeremy on his daily walk. College was open again today but he hadn't felt like going in. They'd probably all still be talking about the attack on that teacher and he didn't want to hear it. A couple of his classmates had already delighted in dwelling on the gory details after the principal had broken the news, casually filling in those that they didn't actually know, and it had made his insides turn over. He had wanted to clap his hands over his ears and shout at them to stop.

The truth was that it had raised the unwelcome memories of the attack on his own mother, Maria. He had been the person who had found her and the image of her lifeless body stretched out across her bed would be etched on his mind forever. All this talk of the attack on Margaret was in danger of ripping the wounds open again, and it would take time to stitch them back up.

Since living with Molly and Jeremy, he had fought hard to recollect only the happy memories of his years with Maria. He had determinedly pushed away the images of his drunken, sweating father staggering around their tiny cramped flat, shouting and swearing while his mother was out at work and his grandfather cowered in the corner. He had forced out the flashbacks to the hot, sultry nights when the sound of gunshots ricocheting around the neighbourhood as rival drug gangs fought for territory was a backdrop to everyday life. They loved their home country but the good times, he knew, had really started when they arrived in the United Kingdom, albeit illegally.

Their existence had been precarious, their status forcing them to live by and large under the radar, but they had been safe and they had each other. For his mother, he knew, the risky and fraught move to the United Kingdom for which she had worked and saved for years had all been about trying to give him better life chances than she had ever had. It still grieved him deeply that she hadn't lived to see him at college. Her own education having been patchy to say the least, it would have been her dream come true.

Sometimes, when the memory of her was particularly strong, it comforted him to think of those evenings together in the small council flat which they had been renting as sub-tenants, unknown to the local authority. The times when they had watched the old British sitcoms on the television, not really understanding the jokes but laughing anyway, sitting on the ancient stained sofa that the previous occupants of the flat had left behind. The Christmases when she had done everything in her power to make things festive, with very little money to do so. And the very best times, when she had cooked feijoada. A Brazilian national dish, it was a rich hearty stew that brought back the very feel of their homeland and which he had determined would be one of the first dishes he would put on the menu when he opened his restaurant.

He had pretended to Molly this morning that he had a sore throat and she had given him a suspicious look, but she hadn't said anything, other than insisting that he take some aspirin. He wasn't missing much at college anyway. It was just one day and he hardly ever took time off. And there was only one lecture this morning and he'd already downloaded the notes from the college intranet. Rubble or one of the others would tell him if he missed anything important. Well, probably not Rubble, who spent most lectures in a fog of affable incomprehension, but one of the others would help him out.

Jeremy, hands in pockets, was deep in thought. As promised, Rubble had got the list of evening class student names for them, but it hadn't really taken them much further. It had simply been a printout of the class register. He sat down on a small wooden bench and pulled it out of his pocket, peering down at the list. He should have remembered to bring his glasses. He looked up as Carlos joined him.

"Any good?" asked Carlos.

"Not really," admitted Jeremy. "I mean it's better than nothing but..." He paused and looked down at the list again. As a teacher, he had been adept at putting names to faces. It was a skill he had developed through necessity. Confronted with several hundred new faces every September, it had been essential to be able to quickly identify individual pupils. Could he do it the other way round though? Could he put faces to names?

He pictured himself back in the classroom that evening, pulling up the mental images and studying them carefully. There had been only one other man beside himself and Mike and so he was easily identified as Nicholas. As far as he could recall, he was a fairly ordinary-looking man, dressed casually in jeans and a sweater who had said very little but had listened attentively, occasionally jotting something down in the notebook he had with him. But there was something about Nicholas... what was it?

He thought harder. It was his eyes. He had very blue eyes. And now he'd remembered that, he could see him clearly in his mind. Satisfied, he scanned the list again. The three older women had sat together and they had definitely known each other. Mike had already identified two of them as Helen and Diana. So that left the final one as Moira. But which was which?

He felt slightly ashamed that he couldn't tell the three women apart. In his mind they all looked pretty much the same. He had once heard his mother say that the older women got the more they became invisible. He thought for a second, momentarily distracted. It looked like she was right. Was it true of older men as well? Probably. He knew that when he was young all his friends' fathers had looked the same to him, in so far as he had looked at them at all. They all wore suits to work, they all polished their shoes and they all drove sensible cars which they cleaned on Sunday mornings. As a teenager, adults had been like a different species and their ways had been a mystery to him.

He smiled to himself. He remembered his father being pleased once when an invitation to a party had been cancelled due to illness. At the time he'd been astonished. Who wouldn't want to go to a party? He understood now, though. In spite of his recent restlessness, his idea of a perfect evening was still to spend it with Molly and Carlos with the cats draped across their laps, watching an old movie and drinking wine. Preferably with the fire lit, the curtains drawn and the outside world being firmly where it belonged. Outside.

He glanced across at Carlos who had got up and was now leaning against a tree, busy scrolling through his phone. Even though his head was bowed so that his face wasn't visible, it was obvious that he was young. Age, he thought, was a great disguise. If he and Carlos committed a crime together, it would be Carlos who would be identified most easily, not him. All he would have to do was wear the ubiquitous chain store sweater and chinos. He could slip into a crowd and melt away. He would be indistinguishable from almost every other middle-aged man.

He glanced down at Aubrey who was sitting by his feet and washing his ears. Did all cats look the same to each other, he wondered? Did they, for instance, know that they were different colours? And if they did, did it matter? Come to that, could they distinguish humans or were they all interchangeable? Surely they could tell one from another, otherwise how would they know who their owners were...

He pulled his thoughts back to his classmates. Interesting though the speculation on cat recognition was, he wanted to present something useful to Mike the next time they met. He thought again about the three women. For some reason his attention was focused on them. Why? A faint memory shivered across his consciousness. Had one of them said or done something that had disturbed him? But what? For the life of him he couldn't remember a single thing that any of them had said. But they must have said something.

Margaret had asked everybody to introduce themselves. They hadn't just sat silently. But it was no good, he had no recollection at all of any of them speaking. He could, just about, see their faces but try as he might he couldn't tell which was which. He thought harder. Yes, he was sure, now he thought about it, that one of them had said something other than her name. She had asked a question about the murdered policeman. Which of them it was, he hadn't got a clue. But it wasn't that which had disturbed him, though. So what was it?

He ran his mind back over the evening. It was towards the end of the class and it was, he was almost sure, when Margaret had started talking about the golf course murders. There had been a change of atmosphere. He had felt it at the time, almost like a tightening of the air they were breathing. Suddenly it came to him. One of the women had looked as though she was in a state of shock. He had glanced across as Margaret was speaking and the woman's face was frozen. She had been staring straight ahead of her and her eyes had been fixed not on Margaret but on the wall behind her. But which one of the women was it? And was it in any way significant?

He stared down at the register again. Why would somebody look so shocked at the mention of the golf course murders? Well, it had been a particularly horrific crime of course but, now he thought about it, it did seem like an extreme reaction. They had all fallen silent, they had all been shocked, but nobody else had looked like that. Was it possible that the woman had known somebody involved in the case? The family of one of the children, perhaps. If she had, she hadn't said anything. But then maybe she wouldn't have wanted to. Maybe the memory was too much. Or was it possible that she knew rather too much, much more than she reasonably ought to have done? He turned the thought over and then leaned down and showed the register to Aubrey.

"What do you reckon, Aubrey?"

Aubrey jumped up beside him and looked at the sheet of paper that Jeremy was holding. Frankly, he didn't reckon anything. He couldn't read. But it was nice to be asked. Whatever was on that sheet was obviously interesting to Jeremy. He must have looked at it about a hundred times already this morning. Aubrey wrapped his tail around himself and settled down. Jeremy sighed.

"Do you think she knew one of those children? Or Harvey? I mean, she looked totally poleaxed."

Maybe she just remembered that she'd left the iron on,

thought Aubrey. Like that memorable time when Jeremy had done just that. Fortunately Carlos had smelled something odd and they had tracked it down to the utility room where the iron's plate was slowly peeling away from the base. He stretched out and rested his paws on Jeremy's knees. Jeremy was good-hearted but not always the most practical of people. It didn't matter. Jeremy made sure they were fed regularly and what more could you ask than that?

Life experience had taught both him and Vincent not to get too fond of humans. They usually let you down. Not always on purpose. Sometimes they just died or got ill, but the end result was the same. For the cat of the house it was either the street or the local rescue centre. But it was difficult not to be fond of Jeremy. After all, it was Jeremy who had rescued him from the Big House that time he'd been banged up. It was Jeremy, along with Molly, who had not only offered him a loving home but had taken in his best mate, Vincent, when he had been in need as well.

He watched as Jeremy folded the register and smoothed it out across his knee. Carlos stuffed his phone back in his pocket and strolled over to join them. Jeremy turned to him.

"I keep looking at the names but they're not really telling me anything."

He reached across and tickled Aubrey's ears.

"I mean, it's just a list."

"Couldn't you, sort of, find out where they all live?"

"I suppose so. We could always check the electoral register but then what would we do? We can't go around stalking them, and even if we did it probably wouldn't take us much further. In fact, it would probably get us arrested."

"We could take it in turns," said Carlos. "And we could wear, like, disguises. That way they wouldn't recognise us."

Jeremy smiled, momentarily distracted by the image of the

pair of them wearing false moustaches with hats pulled down over their eyes. He opened his mouth to say something and then closed it again. Carlos was only trying to be helpful, he knew. For a moment the three of them sat in companiable silence.

"Those old murders and that teacher being attacked and that, it might not be anything to do with any of them anyway," said Carlos eventually. "This all might just be a waste of time."

Aubrey looked at him. He'd changed his tune. It was Carlos who'd said there was a connection in the first place. Now he seemed to be backing away from it. He knew why though. He'd heard him talking to Teddy last night. Carlos rarely mentioned his mother to anybody. Except to Teddy. He talked about her to Teddy.

"I know," said Jeremy. "I keep telling myself that. But, really, even though I keep turning all the possibilities over in my head, I keep coming back to the same conclusion. The attack on Margaret must be connected to the golf course murders. Surely it's connected to what she was talking about that night, to whatever it is she's discovered for the book she's writing. Why else would a perfectly harmless woman be randomly attacked for no apparent reason?"

Carlos thought for a moment.

"It's like that *Sleeping Murder*."

"What?"

Jeremy looked confused.

"*Sleeping Murder*," Carlos repeated. "That old film we watched. That one where the murder was all, like, years ago."

"I think you're right," said Jeremy. "I'm sure this has roots in the past. And you know what they say," continued Jeremy.

"No, what?" said Carlos.

"Old sins have long shadows."

Aubrey rolled onto his side and yawned. He didn't have a clue what Jeremy was talking about. Shadows were just shadows. Who cared if they were long or short? Although, he had to admit, long shadows were more useful for hiding in when necessary. Which it sometimes was.

"What does that mean?" asked Carlos. "What have shadows got to do with it?"

"Well, it means that things that we do in the past sometimes come back to haunt us."

Carlos thought about that. It was true. Like when he and his mother had lived in São Paulo, there had been a man who had taken money from the local shopkeepers and bar owners for what he called protection. He had asked his mother once what he had been protecting people from. She had stroked his head and given him a small, sad smile.

"Danger, Carlos. He is protecting them from danger."

The man had been small and slimy with narrow eyes, bad teeth, and a series of small jagged scars around his mouth. Everybody hated him. But everybody was afraid of him and had paid what he demanded. He had left the area eventually, much to everyone's relief, and gone to live in the countryside. They heard several years later that he had been found with his throat cut and that a number of people had been involved. His murderers were never caught. Some people said that it was because nobody was looking for them.

Jeremy stood up.

"Come on, you two. Let's walk a bit more, I feel the need for fresh air today."

He glanced over to his right.

"I've never been over that way before."

Aubrey glanced with him. Jeremy might not have been over that way before but he and Vincent had, several times. The graves there were newer than the rest of those in the churchyard and had more visitors. They had often seen the same people laying flowers, and sometimes toys, on the graves. Thinking of

Vincent made Aubrey wonder where he had got to this morning. He'd disappeared just after breakfast and he hadn't seen him since. Ah well, no doubt he'd turn up in his own good time.

"This must be the modern part," said Jeremy as they approached the northern end of the graveyard. "Well, I say modern, I mean twentieth century. I suppose if we don't move house again, Molly and me might end up here one day." He stopped and looked about him at the neatly tended graves and carefully pruned shrubs. "I can think of worse places."

Aubrey shivered slightly. So could he. Like being thrown under a hedge or being chucked out with the recycling, like their mate Titan had nearly been. Short for Titanic, Titan attracted disaster. Trapped in the bin which he'd managed to climb into when the wind had lifted the lid and flung it back, he'd been trundled out to the recycling lorry. It was only the quick action of a sharp-eyed binman who had spotted him and lifted him out that had saved him. As Vincent had said at the time, Titan took bad luck to whole new levels. He jumped as he felt a soft shape brush against him. Vincent. Talk of the devil.

"Hello, Vin. What you been up to?"

Vincent shrugged his sleek shoulders.

"This and that. What's he doing?" He nodded his head towards Jeremy, who was now leaning over and reading the inscriptions on the graves.

"Exploring."

Vincent regarded him for a moment and then turned back to Aubrey.

"Right." He paused and gave his right ear a quick wash. "I saw that Clara this morning. Ran into her when I was in the park."

Aubrey waited. It was no good asking Vincent what he'd been doing in the park, he'd tell him if he wanted to. But they both knew Clara. A tiny elderly black cat with small, rather elegant, white paws. She looked as though a puff of wind would blow her over. They first met her when they discovered her sitting on a wall one day, staring anxiously about her and seemingly confused as to where she was. After deducing where she lived from various landmarks she described, they had taken her home and waited until she was securely inside before they'd set off again. As Aubrey had said to Vincent, apart from the fact that it was their duty, it might be one of them one day. Since then they had discovered her in several locations and each time they had escorted her safely home.

"How is she? Is she all right?" Aubrey asked. "Was she lost again?"

Vincent nodded.

"Where was she this time?"

"Sitting on the bandstand," said Vincent. "She didn't have a clue where she was. I took her home and we had a bit of a chat on the way. She's worried about her owner."

"Is she? Why?"

"Clara said that she just seems different. Like distracted. Sort of not herself. And the other day she found her sitting hunched up on the kitchen floor. And," he added, "she forgot to feed her last night."

"No!" said Aubrey. "I mean, forgetting to feed her..." He paused for a moment while he contemplated the horror of a no-show at feeding time. "What happened in the end?"

"Well, she remembered eventually but Clara said that it was really late. She was seriously worried. I mean, it's not like she can just go and get her own anymore."

Aubrey nodded. If it had been him or Vincent and the worst had come to the worst, they would have just hopped in through a neighbouring cat flap, the resident cat wouldn't have minded if they explained the predicament. Or they would have raided a bin somewhere. But Clara really wasn't up to that sort of caper anymore. No wonder she was concerned. And as to her owner sitting around on the floor, that was something that only teenagers did. He'd noticed it with Carlos and Teddy when she came to visit. He'd never seen Molly or Jeremy do it.

"Anyway," continued Vincent. "I had a look at her when I got Clara back. Just through the window."

"And?"

Vincent shrugged.

"Nothing really. She seemed all right. She's quite old though. Not ancient. But..." He paused for a moment. "Yeah, old."

They both fell silent. While elderly people made excellent pet owners, having plenty of spare time to talk to them, feed them, and provide warm laps for them to sit on, there was no denying that they had an unfortunate habit of dying. Which meant the pet or pets in question being placed back in the Big House again. Back on the market and at the mercy of whoever decided to pick them. That's if they were lucky. Sometimes they were just turned out on to the street to fend for themselves. And if the streets in question happened to be in a big town or city, life expectancy was often very short, particularly for older pets. Molly and Jeremy had microchipped both him and Vincent, but they could be microchipped from head to tail, it counted for nothing if there was no home to return you to.

He turned round suddenly, startled at the sound of Jeremy's voice.

"Carlos, look."

The two cats ran over to where Jeremy was standing. Whatever Jeremy had discovered, he sounded excited.

"Look." Jeremy pointed down to three graves set closely together, each with the same-shaped headstone and gold etched lettering. "Look at the dates."

Carlos leaned over to look and then straightened up.

"Do you think…"

"I do. I think that these must be the graves of the children. The golf course children. Look at the dates of their births and deaths. The dates of death of two of them are the same and the other one is just a few days later. It must be them. Why else would three children have died within days of each other? And they're modern graves."

"Somebody's been leaving flowers," he continued. He indicated as he spoke, his hand waving across the small pathetic-looking bunches of flowers, their brittle stems tied together with narrow ribbon and their heads brown and withered. "Not recently by the look of them, but not that long ago."

He fell silent as he contemplated the neat little plots in front of him. This was the thing that these children were remembered for. Not for anything that they'd done in their short lives, but for being dead. For the first time they'd seen their names. Sally, Ruth, and Tommy. Jeremy reached across and gently pulled Carlos's arm down as he raised his phone.

"No, don't do that."

Carlos looked at him, his eyes sombre. He had been going to take a picture to show Teddy, but Jeremy was right. Not everything had to be captured.

"It has given me an idea though," said Jeremy. "You know I mentioned the electoral register earlier?"

"What about it?" asked Carlos, taking a last glance at his phone before he put it back in his pocket.

"I'm sure it must be possible to find historic registers. If we stick with the idea that somebody in the evening class had something to do with the attack on Margaret, a good starting point would be to find out which of them were living in the area at the time of the murders."

CHAPTER FIFTEEN

Jeremy headed instinctively for the same place in which he'd sat the last time. He'd realised years ago that it was what people invariably did, young or old. It brought a sense of security and familiarity to things. It was one of the ways in which he'd managed to learn the names of his own students so quickly, they always headed for the same seat in the classroom. It made it so much easier to identify them. He looked around him now.

The three women were here and, as expected, sitting in the same places as last time. So was Nicholas. Mike would be here soon he knew, having spoken to him on the phone earlier. He was slightly surprised that all of the women had turned up. By and large, he would have thought that women had more to fear from a random attacker than a man on the basis that they were easier targets and less able to fight back. Older women in particular were probably more vulnerable. Also, given the ferocity of the attack on Margaret, there was the underlying fear that it might, somehow, just be the start. After all, it wouldn't be the first time that the town had been caught in the grip of terror.

All in all, he had been expecting the lectures to be cancelled so the emails had come as a complete surprise. The first, from the college principal, had addressed him simply as *Dear Student*. In it she had expressed profound regret with regard to what she had described as the incident on the college campus. She was, she had stressed, anxious to reassure all students that their safety and welfare was of the utmost importance to the college. She wished to emphasise that it continued, in spite of recent events, to be a safe and welcoming environment. Interesting, thought Jeremy, that she had managed to avoid stating what had actually happened. The email had been followed shortly after by a second one from the local history society, which had been addressed to Jeremy and his classmates personally. One of their members had offered to take Margaret's place. Would Jeremy indicate whether he would like the lectures to continue? Jeremy had taken all of ten seconds to do exactly that. It was, whichever way he looked at it, a God-sent opportunity to have another look at his classmates.

In his study, Jeremy sat back in the small armchair and cradled a glass of whisky against his chest while he mulled over the events of the evening. Downstairs he could hear the faint buzz of the television as Molly and Carlos watched some cookery show they had just discovered and to which Carlos was now addicted. Using the excuse of checking a report before he sent it in the morning, he had slipped upstairs with his drink. He wanted to think things over quietly, without being distracted by images of ripe tomatoes and succulent olives accompanied by the sound of Carlos tapping on his tablet and muttering to himself as he jotted down the names of new ingredients.

Overall it had, he thought, been a productive evening. Particularly as Mike had asked everybody to go to the pub after class. What better way to get people to loosen their tongues than over a drink he had said, and Jeremy had agreed. It hadn't been very difficult to persuade them. Even the stand-in lecturer, a tall silver-haired man in his late sixties, had joined them. Deciding on the pub nearest to the college, they had sat at a table in the corner, fairly awkwardly to start with, nursing their drinks and trying to think of something to say. It had been the stand-in lecturer who had broken the ice by asking them what had attracted them to join the course. One of the three women had spoken first, the one that he now knew was called Diana.

She had, she said, been attending evening classes for some time. It was something to do. It saved her from interminable television-watching and aimlessly roaming the internet. And her two friends had nodded in agreement. And, she said, she had always been interested in the history of her hometown. Seizing his opportunity he had asked, trying to sound casual, whether she had always lived in the area? She replied that she had. Although she had travelled quite extensively, she never actually lived anywhere else. He and Mike had tried not to exchange triumphant glances. So, at least one of them had almost certainly been here when the murders had taken place. He had felt slightly less triumphant when her friends had confided that they were all what they called local girls too, having lived in or around the town all their lives. The way things were going, Nicholas probably had family in the area going back to Domesday.

He had turned to Nicholas, more in hope than expectation.

"So, Nicholas, how about you? Are you a local too?"

Nicholas had smiled. He had moved here from another part of the country when he had taken a post here as head librarian for the county about a year ago. Since his divorce he had, he said, taken quite a few evening classes. Jeremy suspected that the motivation to attend evening classes was less about the desire to learn something new and more about the wish to meet new people, perhaps more specifically, new women. And why not, he thought. Working at the county hall with responsibility for libraries was probably hardly conducive to finding a new partner. He associated libraries with rows of regimented shelves, poor lighting, and grim people with tight lips. The latter probably because he'd constantly been told to shut up in his local one when he was a boy. But whatever his motivation for attending the class, Jeremy just couldn't see Nicholas as the person who had committed such a ferocious attack on Margaret. But then, he couldn't see any of the others in that role either.

None of them had stayed at the pub for very long. They were all driving. But it hadn't mattered. What he had wanted was to get a closer look at them all. And he had, focusing particularly on the women. One of them, if only he could remember which, had definitely reacted when the golf course murders had been raised. It wasn't much to go on, but it was something. He'd studied them as they sipped at their glasses of wine. When he looked at them more closely, it really wasn't difficult to see the younger selves that they had been. Diana was slightly taller than the other two, with large blue eyes and a kindly smile. Helen was smaller in stature with softly waving grey hair. Moira had been friendly and chatty, telling the group about their weekly lunches and coach trips to stately homes, which, she said, they were ticking off of a list.

In essence they were three perfectly agreeable older women, friends who enjoyed attending evening classes together and generally kept themselves busy to stave off the boredom of old age. Was it really possible that one of them could have committed such a vicious attack on Margaret? He just couldn't see one of these kindly, friendly women bringing a blunt instrument down on Margaret's head with such force that she was still in hospital.

And was he being too hasty in dismissing Nicholas? Just because he was a librarian, it didn't mean that he wasn't capable of such an act. Or was he just being a total twat and engaging in some kind of Boy's Own detective adventure simply because he was restless and bored? He was beginning to suspect the latter.

It had been Mike, turning to the women, who had raised the topic of the golf course murders again.

"I expect you all remember the case that Margaret was talking about? The golf course one?"

"Yes, it was dreadful." It was Moira who spoke, the light catching on her delicately tinted red hair. "It practically brought the town to a standstill, didn't it?"

She turned to her two friends for confirmation.

"Dreadful," agreed Helen. "Everybody was under suspicion. It was like some awful nightmare."

"But they never caught anyone?" persisted Mike.

"No," agreed Diana. "They never caught anyone."

Jeremy had held his breath and then plunged in. There might not be another opportunity.

"Margaret seemed to think that she knew something about the case. Some new evidence or something." He kept his tone deliberately light. "I mean, something she found out for the book that she's writing."

He had dipped his head to his pint and watched them over the rim of his glass. Not one of them had changed expression. They had all looked simply mildly curious, including Nicholas, and then the lecturer had changed the subject by asking whether any of them had thought of joining the local history society, which welcomed new members. He had fought down his irritation. Tempting though it was, he couldn't just switch back to the murders. It would make him look not only ghoulish but weird. Shortly afterwards, they had finished their drinks and left, tacitly agreeing that they would walk back to the college car park together. Although, he reflected now, it was entirely possible that one of their number had nothing to fear.

Jeremy drained his glass and sat forward, resting his elbows on his knees. He wasn't sure that what he'd learned tonight was particularly useful but at least it was a start. It was better than nothing. It was annoying that he still couldn't identify which of the women had looked so shocked when Margaret raised the golf club murders but it would come to him eventually. He parked it at the back of his mind. It had been such a fleeting impression and experience had taught him that on the occasion when he really wanted to remember something, it nearly always eluded him, only to drift to the surface in a totally unexpected moment. He'd let his subconscious work on it. Something would jog his memory.

So what was the next step? The obvious thing would be to ask Margaret what it was that she had found out but according to Carlos, who had heard it at college, she was still in hospital and still unconscious. And even if she regained consciousness, he could hardly hang around at her bedside badgering her for information. A thought suddenly struck him. What if her injury had caused her to suffer long-term memory loss? What if she never recalled what she had found out? He'd read about cases where people had been involved in some kind of accident and were then found wandering, with no idea of who they were or even where they were. No, he was letting his imagination run away with him. Even in the worst-case scenario, even if she never recalled so much as her own name, Margaret was a former journalist. Any research that she had undertaken would be stored somewhere, electronically as well as on hard copy.

He stood up and pulled out a fresh new notebook from the small stack he kept on a shelf. Sitting back down he flicked it open as he tried to clear his mind. Like most people, he used his laptop to create documents. In fact, when it came to work it was essential. So much so that he could barely remember the old days when posting meant putting something in an envelope with a stamp on it. But when he needed to really think something through, when he wanted to just think freely, he needed a pen and paper. Even if he created a Word document later, there was something about physically forming the words in his own slightly scruffy handwriting that gave cohesion to his thoughts.

He rested his thumb on the top of his pen and clicked slowly up and down while he thought things through. What if he was entirely wrong about all of this? What if the attack on Margaret had been completely random or there had been some motive that he couldn't even begin to guess? Even as the thought came up for air, he dismissed it. The golf course murders were, he was still sure, at the heart of this. Every instinct told him that they were the reason for the attack on Margaret. That would, surely, be the best place to start.

So what did he know about the victims? Know for a fact rather than speculation. Well, he knew that three children had been involved, two girls and one boy, and following the walk in the churchyard he now knew their names. He also knew that the boy had been killed later than the girls. Why? Because Tommy was some kind of threat? Or perhaps the killer was just randomly targeting children and Tommy had the serious misfortune to be in the wrong place at the wrong time, just as the two girls had been. Or, was it perhaps possible that Tommy had been killed by someone else entirely?

Jeremy started to dismiss the thought and then pulled it back. There were such things as copycat crimes, he knew. Was it within the realms of possibility that there had been another unhinged killer on the block? Hadn't Sherlock Holmes said that once you eliminate the impossible, whatever remains, no matter how improbable, must be the truth? Well, it wasn't impossible that there had been two murderers on the patch so it couldn't be entirely dismissed. He bent over the notepad and began scribbling.

Two minutes later he sat back and reviewed what he had written. It was precious little. The names of the children, with a question mark against Tommy's, when they had been killed, the ages they had been, and where they had been found. There was also the question of motive. He knew how the children had been killed, what he didn't know was why. And why had the killings suddenly stopped? There must be more information out there, something that might give some clue. Mike had, he knew already, done quite a lot of research. Perhaps he'd wait until they spoke again before he did any more. There was no point in repeating what Mike had already done.

He turned his thoughts away from the children and towards the murderer and began writing again.

The murderer of the children had been male. At least, that was what the police had thought. The only male in the evening class apart from himself and Mike was Nicholas. But Nicholas was the wrong age to have committed the murders. He was probably a similar age at the time to the children who had been killed and while children had been known to kill other children they had generally been brought swiftly to justice. Which left the women. He paused and lifted his pen from the page. They had all lived in the town at the time. Maybe one of them had been some kind of accomplice. Somebody who didn't actually commit the deed but was in some way involved. It wasn't beyond the bounds of possibility.

He let the thought filter through his brain. How likely was it that a woman had played a part in the murders? It was a horrible thought but almost before it had finished forming, the well-known images of two women who had assisted their male partner in the murder of children sprang to the forefront of his mind. But they were the exception rather than the rule, which was probably why society found them so abhorrent. Generally, he was sure, fewer women than men committed murder and, of those, very few indeed killed children.

Nevertheless, while it seemed unlikely that a woman had been involved in the golf course murders, following the Holmesian theory, it couldn't be entirely discounted. He'd already discussed with Mike the possibility of the perpetrator of the attack on Margaret being a woman, why not take that a stage further and implicate her in the actual murders? Jotting down the word 'woman' with a question mark, he turned his thoughts again to the people in his evening class.

The obvious thing to do was Google them all. Most people turned up there eventually, if the searcher was patient enough. Very few people managed to live completely under the digital radar. And, luckily, due to Rubble and the register, he had the complete names of his classmates. He would start with the three women.

He moved across to his desk and switched on his laptop. Fifteen minutes later he sat back and looked at his notes. All he had discovered from Google was that Diana played golf and had won a local tournament, Helen was on the committee of a local gardening club, and Moira had sung in a local choir last Christmas. He sighed. Three ordinary women leading three ordinary lives. All right, Diana had a connection to the golf club but then so did hundreds of other people, including himself.

He turned back to the screen. He might as well check out Nicholas, too, while he was about it. Flicking his fingers quickly across the keyboard he typed in his name and the word libraries. Within a split second it appeared on the screen, along with a photograph and his title. Nicholas Shaw, Head of Library Services, and beneath it a short résumé, courtesy of the local authority website. He ran his eye over it, noting the various posts that Nicholas had held. Nothing much there... and then he stopped and leaned in closer, a flush of excitement running through him. While what Nicholas had said about himself in the pub was, strictly speaking, true, it wasn't the whole picture. Nicholas had taken up his current post from another county a year ago but that county wasn't his home. He had been born here, right in this town, and he had lived here until he was eighteen.

CHAPTER SIXTEEN

Jeremy stared at the screen, his thoughts buzzing. If Nicholas was roughly the same age as the children who were killed, it was entirely possible that he had known them. He might even have attended the same school, gone to the same children's parties, perhaps played games in the park with them. Given their similarity in age, even if he didn't know them personally he must have at least known what had happened to them. There couldn't have been a person in the town who didn't, and the children would have been particularly afraid. For many of them it would have been their first experience of the finality of death and, as experiences go, it would have been a pretty dreadful one. For most, himself included, their first confrontation with death comes when they're adults, and then it's often a grandparent or other elderly relative that has died. Such deaths, while sad, are not usually totally unexpected.

The experience of the town's children had been the complete opposite. They had been suddenly pushed face to face with the brutally shocking and permanent removal of some of their playmates. Carlos had said that his friend's mother had told her that all the children were terrified that summer and that their parents had practically put them under house arrest. Surely Nicholas must have been among them? So why had he lied? He corrected himself. To be fair, Nicholas hadn't actually lied. He had simply been what his father would have called economical with the truth.

He ran his thoughts over this evening's conversation again, mentally hitting the replay button in his head. What had Nicholas actually said? He had said, he was sure, that he had moved here from another area to take up the post of Head of Library Services which, strictly speaking, was true. What he hadn't said was that he was no stranger to the town. The result was that they had all been left with the impression that he wasn't local. When they were all talking about where they had come from, surely the obvious thing for Nicholas to say would have been that while he had recently moved to the area, he had in fact been born here. That it wasn't so much a move as a homecoming. But he hadn't. Why not? Perhaps he was just a private sort of person. Someone who didn't like sharing personal details. He could understand that. He wasn't keen on oversharing himself. But what would have been the harm in at least saying that he was back in his hometown?

He scrolled down the screen but nothing else about Nicholas appeared, other than a short news piece about the return of mobile libraries in the rural areas. In fact, the information about all of his classmates was frustratingly thin. He pushed his chair back and got up. While Google had produced some results, it wasn't really anything that he could use. Apart from joining Helen's gardening club or Moira's choir, which would start to look distinctly like stalking, he couldn't really get any further. All four of his classmates were annoyingly elusive.

He walked over to the window and opened it. Outside, the night was cold and still. The local authority had taken the cost-cutting measure of turning off street lamps after ten o'clock, in spite of local protests, and on nights like this the only illumination on the residential streets was from the stars. While Jeremy agreed that turning off the lamps compromised the safety of the residents, he had to admit that on nights like this, the cold beauty of the stars glittering against the darkness was breathtaking. Across to the west he could hear the distant steady stream of cars, their lights twinkling like strings of diamonds as they made their way along the bypass. The bypass was relatively new, it hadn't been built when the murders had taken place. But the stars... the stars had been here forever.

He turned to face the room and leaned back against the windowsill. The faces of his classmates danced before him. How could he find out more about them? There must be some way. Private investigators did it all the time. Except that he wasn't a private investigator. He was just an ordinary bloke who was a bit fed up and who was, in reality, meddling in things that were nothing to do with him. He felt suddenly depressed. Perhaps he ought to just take up a new hobby. Something sensible though. Not like their erstwhile neighbour Dan who, on the occasion of his fiftieth birthday, had bought himself a Harley Davidson and started dressing himself in tight leathers, much to the amusement of the local teenagers. And the chagrin of his wife.

Anyway, he didn't want a Harley Davidson. Fantastic piece of motor engineering though they were, big bikes just weren't him. The trouble was that he didn't really know what *was* him. When he was a boy he had collected stamps, in fact, he'd been quite an enthusiast. Perhaps he'd start that again. He was sure he still had his albums somewhere, either here or at his parents' house. He could make a start by digging them out. There was bound to be a local or online group that he could join. He jumped as his mobile vibrated on his desk. He picked it up and glanced down. A text. Probably some non-existent delivery company who urgently needed paying for a parcel that nobody had sent him. It was Mike.

Interesting evening tonight. Definitely worth doing a bit more digging.

Suddenly his low mood evaporated. Mike was right, it had been an interesting evening. So why shouldn't they do a bit of sleuthing if they wanted to? It wasn't hurting anybody and they might even uncover something important. And Mike was an ex-copper, he wasn't exactly an amateur.

He looked up as Carlos put his head round the door. Jeremy smiled at him. For all his attempts at sophistication, including the fashionable clothes that he bought with his allowance from Molly and Jeremy and the wages he earned from his part-time job as assistant chef at Lilac Tree Lodge care home, there still hung about him the ghost of the shy gentle boy with the badly cut hair and cheap trainers that he had been when he first joined Sir Frank's.

"Have you finished your report?"

"Just about. Carlos, if you wanted to find out something about somebody, how would you do it?"

Carlos sidled round the door and into the room, followed by Aubrey who slipped in after him. Jeremy's study was one of Aubrey's favourite places but he needed to keep a low profile at the moment, having recently been chucked out for jumping up at a fly and knocking a mug of coffee over some papers on Jeremy's desk.

"It's obvious," said Carlos.

"Is it?"

Carlos nodded and pulled out his phone from his pocket.

"Who do you want to find out about?"

Jeremy picked up the evening class register which had been sitting on his desk and passed it to him.

"This lot."

Carlos glanced at it.

"Facebook probably. Because they're all, like, old."

Of course. Facebook. It was obvious. Everybody used Facebook. Well, everybody except him. Jeremy watched as Carlos sat forward on the armchair, phone in one hand, register in the other. Interesting, he thought, how youngsters used their thumbs to navigate small keyboards. He still used his fingers, prodding away one letter at a time. Perhaps one day thumbs would evolve with usage, become huge by comparison to fingers. Would people in the future stare at images of twenty-first century people and wonder how they ever managed to navigate the world with their little tiny thumbs? Perhaps they wouldn't. Perhaps all the screens would be implanted in their brains. Would that mean that they would have to charge their heads? Would there be public head-charging stations? And would there still be things like Facebook?

He knew what Facebook was, of course, but he'd never really used it. When he was teaching, he had always felt that getting caught up in social media would be a foolish thing to do. He'd seen too many younger colleagues come to grief, caught out by savvy students who had easily accessed their posts and then shared them among their mates. The worst case had been Sam, the young science teacher who had thought it was a good idea to post a picture of his bare bum at a party. The image had been shared round the school almost before Sam had time to pull his trousers up. Unsurprisingly, Sam was subsequently unable to establish any authority in the classroom, and had left shortly after. In Jeremy's opinion, teaching brought enough challenges, especially at a school like Sir Frank's, without trying to navigate the tricky path of Facebook or Instagram. It was easier to just stay away from it altogether. So much so that it had pretty much passed him by. But now he thought about it, it definitely had its benefits. Mike used social media, he knew. He had mentioned the Facebook group set up by local police. He leaned forward as Carlos turned his phone screen towards him.

"Do you recognise any of these?"

Jeremy peered more closely. It was no good, the screen was too small. He passed his tablet to Carlos.

"Can you do it on this? I can't see properly on the small screen."

Carlos nodded.

"Course. Just give me a minute to find it and log in."

Jeremy watched his dark head bent over the screen when a thought suddenly struck him. If Facebook was for old people, why did Carlos have an account?

"Carlos." He spoke slowly. If the boy didn't want to tell him then that was fine. It was actually none of his business, but he was curious. "What do you use Facebook for?"

Carlos looked up, fingers hovering over the screen, and swallowed hard. He looked suddenly vulnerable.

"It's my mum. And my dad."

"Your mum and dad?" Jeremy was confused. They knew for a fact that Maria was dead, and he'd always had the impression that Carlos's father was too. Why did Carlos think that he'd find them on Facebook?

"I've been sort of looking for them." Carlos hesitated for a moment and then ploughed on. "Well, my dad really. Mum didn't use social media. We didn't have the internet at the flat. Or in Brazil," he added. "I mean, it was there. It's just that we didn't have it."

Carlos kept his head down as he talked. Jeremy knew very well why they didn't have the internet. They had barely enough money to feed and clothe themselves. They certainly couldn't have afforded a luxury like the internet.

Sensing the change in Carlos's mood, Aubrey padded across from the other side of the room where he'd tucked himself under the radiator, and jumped onto the arm of his chair. Tentatively stretching a paw, he reached across and patted the tablet. It always made Carlos smile when he did that. It made him smile, too. He liked seeing the pictures jump about, especially when they were cat videos which Jeremy sometimes showed him when he was in a good mood. In fact, he'd discussed cat videos with Vincent recently when they'd tried to work out how to summon them up themselves. But it was no good, they couldn't crack it.

"Mum always said that Dad was probably dead," Carlos continued, gently removing Aubrey's paw. "But we didn't know for sure. He just disappeared and we never heard from him again. To be honest, it was a couple of weeks before we even noticed that he hadn't come back. I mean, he was always going off and then he'd just turn up again. But that time, he didn't. But we never got any, like, confirmation that something had happened to him. So I started thinking that maybe he could still be out there somewhere. I thought that if he was still alive and if he used any stuff, it would be Facebook. Because of his age and that."

"And did you? Find him?"

Carlos looked up from the screen.

"Sort of. I found a Facebook group from our old neighbourhood in São Paulo. There were some pictures that someone had posted. Old pictures that were taken during the carnival."

"What was the carnival like?" Jeremy asked, suddenly interested. England didn't really have a tradition of carnivals apart from Notting Hill. He'd never visited it, but from footage he'd seen there always seemed to be an atmosphere of fun and excitement. All right, it had, he knew, its darker moments but what event didn't? He didn't think that Molly would like it, she wasn't great with crowds, but maybe he'd take Carlos this summer. He made a mental note to mention it to him later.

Carlos put the tablet to one side for the moment, one hand gently stroking Aubrey, his expression thoughtful as he relived the memories of his childhood.

"Carnival in São Paulo was great, it was really exciting. It wasn't the biggest though. The biggest carnival was Rio de Janeiro, that's the one that you always see pictures of on the telly and that. But ours was good, too. Everybody looked forward to it. We all used to go together, even Grandad. But Dad always used to get drunk and then we wouldn't see him for days," he added flatly.

He picked up the tablet again and flicked his thumbs quickly across the screen.

"Look. I think that might be him."

And Jeremy found himself looking at Carlos. An older Carlos who was clearly the worse for wear, laughing, glass in hand, leaning back against a wall. But the likeness was unmistakeable. Tall and dark, with laughing brown eyes, it wasn't difficult to understand what Maria had seen in him. Any young woman would have been swayed by such a handsome man. He didn't look particularly intelligent, but since when had teenaged girls taken that into account? Or teenaged boys for that matter. Many a young marriage had later foundered on the rocks of intellectual incompatibility. He'd seen it with one or two of his own school friends. And, when all was said and done, Maria had at least gained Carlos.

He found himself suddenly wondering what would have happened to Carlos if he had stayed in Brazil. It wasn't something that he'd really thought about before. Carlos had become so much a part of his home with Molly and the cats that sometimes it seemed like he'd always been with them. A time when he'd lived a different life in a different country seemed almost unimaginable.

He stared down at the images of Carlos's father. Would Carlos have turned out like him if his mother hadn't been determined to get him to the United Kingdom? Would he have been unable to resist the lure of alcohol? He'd heard it said that alcoholism was hereditary, that some people were predisposed to it. If opportunities for Carlos had been limited, as surely they would have been given his distinctly inauspicious start in life, then maybe a descent into some kind of addiction would have been inevitable.

But Maria, although loud, unpredictable, and aggressive, had also been hard-working, tenacious, and determined to make something of her son's life. So it was just as likely that Carlos had inherited her strengths rather than his father's weaknesses. He felt suddenly cheered. All the evidence to date suggested that Carlos had done exactly that. He'd achieved good results at school and worked hard at college. He didn't go out with his friends and come home rolling drunk, or worse. He was a nice, friendly, courteous lad. But above all, he had ambition and he had, surely, inherited that from his mother. Carlos's dream was, he knew, to own a restaurant and so far everything seemed to point to him being able to achieve just that.

He eyed his foster son affectionately. What Carlos didn't know was that he and Molly had already talked about giving him a hand setting up when the time came, a conversation that Aubrey had listened to with interest. Aubrey knew what a restaurant was, having had several on his evening rounds at their last house and having made sure to ingratiate himself with one or two of the local ones when they had first moved here. If Carlos was going to have one of his own then that was surely going to be a win for him and Vincent. He already fed them scraps from the kitchen when they visited Lilac Tree Lodge. Who knew what they might get if he had free reign?

"I was just curious," said Carlos. "Sort of wondering about him and that. What he was like. I didn't really know him. I was only about five when he disappeared. I did get a birthday card from him once, but that was all."

"It's perfectly natural to be curious," said Jeremy. "I think I would have felt the same."

"Would you?" Carlos smiled suddenly, the light dancing in his eyes. "Honestly?"

"Honestly," said Jeremy. "I think most people would like to know at least something about their lineage."

"Their what?"

Carlos looked at him suspiciously.

"Lineage," said Jeremy. "It just means where you came from. Sort of."

"Right." Carlos nodded. Another new word to impress Teddy with. "Only I thought you might think I was being stupid if I told you I'd been looking for him. Because of what he was like and that."

"I'm sure that he wasn't always a..." Jeremy searched for the right words. He had been going to say useless drunk. Although that might have been the truth, some things were better not said, and he was still Carlos's father. "Troubled man," he continued. "I mean, there must have been something good about him. After all, your mother married him."

He resisted the temptation to add that she had probably been too young to know any different. But it was perfectly natural for Carlos to search for his father, in his position he would probably have done the same. But how amazing that he had actually found him. Well, found pictures of him anyway. That's what modern technology could do. No more slogging round old newspaper archives, no more driving miles to some far-off county and squinting over parish records. There, by the wonder of the internet, was the whole world. Including São Paulo. And including three women and a man whose names he now had.

CHAPTER SEVENTEEN

From the roof of the bus shelter where they'd been observing a learner drive stuttering and stalling along the quiet road, Aubrey and Vincent turned as Clara pattered into view. They watched her put a tentative paw to the road surface.

Vincent turned to Aubrey and sighed.

"Come on, she'll get killed like that."

Leaping gracefully down they ran towards her. She looked up at them, her small pretty face etched in confusion.

"All right, Clara?"

Aubrey glanced sideways at his friend. For all his streetwise ways and air of independence, Vincent could be surprisingly gentle when he chose. He had been the same with Buster, the small golden puppy that they had once rescued from a caravan site. There was definitely a side to Vincent that wasn't always obvious.

Clara sat down on the pavement and stared at them, apparently unable to think of anything to say.

"Do you think we ought to take her home, Vin?" Aubrey asked.

Vincent nodded.

"I reckon. We can't leave her here. She's not safe. It's only round the corner anyway."

Standing one each side of her they gently nudged her to her feet. The streets were quiet at this time of day but there was still traffic around. It would only take a hit from one car that braked too late to snuff out Clara's fragile little life.

Together, the three of them padded slowly forward, Aubrey and Vincent matching their pace to Clara's. Turning left at the top of the road they made their way to Clara's house.

"Better see her in," said Vincent.

Aubrey nodded. He wasn't sure how with it Clara actually was. They couldn't just leave her outside, she wouldn't be safe. Although she had her good days, it didn't look like today was one of them. She seemed to be completely unsure of where she was. She could easily just wander off again and get injured in some way. She might not have much life left, but what she had she was entitled to.

Guiding her down the path towards the back door and the cat flap, they suddenly stopped and sniffed the air. Aubrey turned to Vincent.

"Funny time to light a fire, Vin."

Vincent nodded.

"Odd."

Wordlessly they crept forward. After a moment's hesitation Clara followed them. At the bottom of the garden, a woman was poking with a stick at a small fire that had been lit inside a metal bin. They dived under a hedge as the woman turned to face them. Clara looked around her uncertainly, puzzled as to where her friends had suddenly disappeared, and then trotted towards the woman, tail in the air.

"Clara. There you are. I've been worried about you. Where on earth have you been?"

Aubrey watched for a moment, head on one side.

"Vin..." He paused. "Do you think that there's something odd about her?"

"She's just old, that's all. Bit confused. Gets to us all in the end. She'll be all right now she's home."

Aubrey shook his head.

"No, not Clara. The woman that's lit the fire."

Vincent narrowed his eyes and considered for a moment.

"Odd in what way?"

"She doesn't seem too steady on her feet."

They watched as the woman staggered slightly and then reached down for a blue book lying on the grass. Picking it up with the tips of her fingers she flung it onto the fire. The flames licked up and caught the pages, wrapping around the photographs that had tumbled out, sending small glowing cinders floating into the air. The woman stood back and watched for a moment, her face expressionless.

"I'm glad you're here," she said, turning again to Clara who had been sitting quietly watching her. "I could do with some company."

She stepped backwards and then sat down suddenly on the grass, one hand clutching an empty carrier bag. Reaching into the pocket of her jacket with the other, she pulled out a small bottle and took a swig from it. She smiled at Clara, a small, sad smile that made the crinkle of the skin around her eyes deeper.

"I should have done this years ago." She licked her lips and wiped her mouth with the back of her hand. "I always knew that it was somewhere in the house. I just didn't know where. He moved it out of his desk right after the golf course murders. But I never looked for it, not really. I suppose if I'm honest, I didn't want to find it. Part of me was just relieved that he'd put it somewhere else. I could pretend that it didn't exist. Some of the time anyway," she added.

She leaned back on her elbows and stared into the distance.

Clara padded towards her and settled herself on her lap.

"But I always knew it was there. I knew that he wouldn't have got rid of anything, not really. Sometimes, when we were just watching television, I'd find myself wondering where he'd put it. It was like having a great malevolent spider in the house, crouching over us and waiting to strike. I could almost feel it spinning its webs with those horrible, long, spindly legs. Even nice days, like birthdays and Christmas, it hung over us." She paused and took another swig from the bottle. "I used to dream about spiders. Sometimes I still do."

Aubrey exchanged a glance with Vincent. They both quite liked spiders. There was something calming about them. Except when they started running of course, but they didn't do any harm. They weren't like rats or cockroaches. But humans didn't like them, he knew. In fact, last autumn Carlos had appeared white-faced in the kitchen and pleaded with Jeremy to remove a particularly large specimen from the windowsill in his bedroom. Aubrey had gone with him, followed by Carlos, Molly, and Vincent. He'd been hoping that the spider in question wasn't Boris who had, unbeknown to the occupants, been living in the house for some time. He needn't have worried. By the time they had all trooped up the stairs and reached the bedroom, the spider had gone. Although Carlos did sleep with the lights on that night. Poor Carlos. Aubrey could have told him that Boris wouldn't hurt a fly. All right, maybe he would hurt a fly. But he wouldn't hurt Carlos. If only Carlos knew, Boris was far more scared of him than the other way round.

He settled down on to his front paws and listened as the woman continued talking to Clara, who was now struggling to keep her eyes open.

"Even though I tried not to, I'd sometimes find myself thinking about it all, re-reading that diary in my mind and wondering, if I found it, if I'd find the courage to destroy it. I didn't think that he'd have taken it into work, that would be far too risky, somebody could easily come across it. A cleaner or a secretary or someone. It wouldn't be in the car or garage either. There was always the chance that me or the children would find it. No, it had to be somewhere in the house. My guess for a long time was that it was still in his study. Some secret place that only he knew about. Somewhere he had easy access, anyway. He'd lived in this house since he was born. He knew every nook and cranny like the back of his hand."

The woman looked down at the back of her own hand as she spoke.

"I wonder why we say that. Why do we assume that everybody knows the back of their hand better than any other part of themselves? I mean, why not the palm?"

Aubrey looked over at Vincent.

"Search me," said Vincent.

"I've read a lot about people like him," the woman continued. "They're called narcissists." She paused for a moment. "I'd never heard that word before. It means somebody who is completely at the centre of their own universe, somebody who always puts themselves first. Other people don't really matter to them. It comes from Greek mythology. I looked it up. There was a boy, the son of some god or other, who was very beautiful. So beautiful that he stared into a pool and fell in love with his own reflection. When I was a teenager, if there was somebody who thought they were a bit special, we used to say, 'I know somebody who fancies him. Himself.' We thought that was hilarious."

She laughed and then her face hardened again and she took another pull on the bottle.

"But people like that, Clara, they're born like it. They don't change. They only see other people in relation to themselves. Even his own children. If they hadn't been successful and clever, if they'd failed at school or been useless at sport, if he hadn't been able to show off about them, if he hadn't seen them as just a reflection of himself, I wonder if he would have felt differently towards them. I think he would. He wouldn't have been so keen to take them to the tennis club for a start."

Vincent turned to Aubrey.

"Like Jester," he said.

Aubrey nodded. While Jester hadn't been known to frequent the tennis club, he had, as the woman had so eloquently expressed it, fancied himself. Being a pedigree, he chose only to make friends with other pedigree cats in the neighbourhood. The one time he had attended a local meet he had sat aloof, occasionally running a sleek paw across one ear and yawning in a studied gesture of boredom. It hadn't done him much good though. The last Aubrey heard, he was in a rescue centre, his owners having separated and neither of them willing to take him. He listened harder as the woman continued talking.

"I wonder sometimes too about his first wife. I knew he was divorced. I asked him about her once. He just said that it had been a mistake and that was it. He never mentioned her again, so I didn't either. I did try to find her once but you know, it's quite difficult to trace women. They get married and change their names. I'm not sure why I wanted to find her, anyway. I mean, what would I have said to her?"

For several moments the two sat in silence. Clara, safe and comfortable in her owner's arms, began gently drifting off to sleep. The woman leaned forward and planted a tiny kiss on Clara's soft little head. She dropped her voice to a whisper. Aubrey inched forward so that he could hear properly.

"Once he was gone, I made up my mind that I really would have to do something about it all. Because of Jack and Anna. You see, if anything were to happen to me, they would have to clear the house and they would be bound to find the diary. And the photographs. They would know that they belonged to their father." Her mouth tightened. "And I couldn't allow that to happen. I just couldn't. Whatever I thought of him, whatever he was and whatever he'd done, I couldn't let the children suffer for it. He was their father and they loved him. But I kept putting it off. It was always next week. Next month. When I was less busy. When I was in the right mood. Like there's ever a right mood. Funnily enough, it's something that the problem pages don't prepare you for."

The woman screwed her eyes shut as if she was in pain. She sat perfectly still for several seconds and then flicked her eyes open again and swallowed hard, as though the words billowing up inside her were pushing to get out before she was ready. Slowly, she began to speak.

"I suppose, in a way, I ought to thank Margaret. If it hadn't been for her and her damned book, who knows how much longer I would have put it off. I might have left it too late. But once I made my mind up, I was determined to go through with it. I started with the obvious place, his study. I was wrong about that though."

She leaned forward and spoke softly into Clara's ear, running her hand across the little cat's back and holding her gently to her.

"You'll never guess where I found it in the end." She paused and gripped Clara a little more tightly. "In the attic. Stuffed into an old leather briefcase of his and tucked under some pipework, right at the back. The funny thing is, I wasn't even looking for it. I only went up there to see if I could find anything for Anna. She's been researching some family history and she'd got quite a lot of information on my side of the family but very little on her father's. And to be honest, there wasn't much I could tell her. I never met his parents. I'd seen photographs of them but they died years ago. Anyway, I thought that if there was anything, any old birth or death certificates, any letters or things like that, they would be in the attic. He came back here after his parents died and all their personal things were still here. He'd updated the furniture and put in a new kitchen and bathroom and so on but I came across the odd thing from time to time. His father's antique paper knife that his patients had given him when he retired and that he kept in his study, a little manicure set which I guess belonged to his mother that I found at the back of the airing cupboard, just small personal items."

For a moment the woman fell silent again and stared into the distance. The sound of the alternating syllables of the chiffchaff resonated on the cold spring air as it flitted through the shrubs. When she spoke her voice sounded stronger.

"That's when I spotted the briefcase. One of those old-fashioned barrel-shaped brown leather ones. I knew before I even opened it what was in it. It was a kind of sixth sense." She laughed suddenly, a grim chortle that held not even a hint of mirth. "No wonder he was so keen to get a loft ladder. All he had to do was wait until I went out shopping or something and then he could just climb up there and pull the ladder after him. Of course, he'd added to it since the last time I saw it." Lying full stretch on the grass she stared up at the scudding clouds. "There was a lock on the briefcase and, do you know, for a moment it floored me. And then I realised. He wasn't there. He wasn't ever going to be there. I could do what I liked. So I went down to the garage, found a heavy screwdriver and levered the lock off."

She took a final swig from the bottle and dropped it beside her.

"It's been five years now since he's been gone. Best five years of my life. If Margaret really has discovered something, they won't find anything here."

Closing her eyes she drifted off into sleep.

CHAPTER EIGHTEEN

Jeremy leaned back in his chair and let out a sigh of contentment. Even though he mostly worked from home now, there was still something special about a Saturday. It was probably a hangover from his youth. Sundays were all about getting ready for school the next day and remembering where you'd chucked your school tie after ripping it off on Friday afternoon. They were about eating too much Sunday lunch and then listening to the top forty on the radio and trying to record it on to a cassette tape. They were about watching the hours tick down until bedtime with the dreaded Monday morning and double geography hard on its heels.

Saturdays, on the other hand, signalled freedom and hours of possibilities. Saturdays were about stooging around in record shops with your mates and flicking through the vinyl. They were about sitting for hours in the Wimpy and then trying to get served in one of the local pubs. Saturdays were about being young.

It was a pity that, as manager, Molly had to go into work today to sort some problems out but she'd be back later. Maybe they'd go into town and have a pizza or something and Carlos too, if he felt like it. He glanced across at Carlos now, his dark head bent over a recipe book, ears hooked to his phone as usual. He wondered what he was listening to. When Jeremy was a teenager, he had listened to his favourite music on a record player in his bedroom, usually at volume, which meant that everybody else had the delight of listening to it as well. Including his father who had frequently shouted up the stairs to turn that bloody racket down. But nowadays there was no way of knowing what youngsters were subjecting themselves to. Their listening was mostly done in a closed world that only they had access to. Carlos could have been listening to Nazi rallying cries for all he knew. Unlikely though.

He picked up the tablet again and continued scrolling. There was no denying, this stuff was addictive. Like human catnip. Determined not to fall down the rabbit hole of social media he had found himself in a quandary this morning. He wanted access to the information that it held but he didn't want accounts of his own. He'd half thought about asking Carlos if he could use his accounts but it didn't seem right, although he was sure that Carlos would have agreed if he'd been asked. He'd tried to get round it by just Googling the names again but the searches had only yielded what he already knew. He had just been going round in circles. It was so frustrating. That they all had Facebook accounts, he knew. Carlos had quickly discovered that for him last night. He just couldn't access them.

He'd talked to Molly about it over breakfast. While never claiming to be technically minded, Molly often came up with a solution when he hit a brick wall. Even if it was of the 'turn it off and on again' variety, which had worked surprisingly often. This morning she had simply handed him her tablet along with the Lilac Tree Lodge password and the information that Lilac Tree Lodge had both Facebook and Instagram accounts which he was welcome to access. He had been amazed. He knew, obviously, that institutions had websites. It was practically obligatory in the twenty-first century, but it had never occurred to him that they had social media accounts as well.

Molly had laughed at his surprise. It was, she explained, one of the ways in which the Lodge engaged with the outside world. It was quick, easy and considerably cheaper than using a public relations firm. All the residents had their own tablet as well, which the Lodge provided for them and encouraged them to use. And after some initial resistance most of them did, from messaging family and friends to playing games, reading their daily newspaper and listening to audio books. The introduction of the tablets had been, said Molly, an outstanding success.

Settling down to it when Molly had left for work, Jeremy had discovered it wasn't difficult to get the hang of it all. Somewhere at the back of his mind he'd had the idea that it was complicated, that you had to be tech savvy to navigate your way round it. Either that, or get a twelve-year-old to explain it. In fact, it turned out to be remarkably easy. Once you'd logged in, you just searched for whoever you were looking for and usually you could see what they'd written, as well as their profile. There was though, he had to admit, something faintly voyeuristic about it. Like peeping in through the window of someone else's house. But, he reasoned, if people didn't want the public to have access to personal information then they shouldn't post it.

He had quickly found what he was looking for. All three of the women had written short profiles and all had given their status as widowed. That made sense, he supposed. It was possibly what had brought them together. He reached across for his notebook and grabbed a pen. It was something else to add to his notes. Running backwards and forwards between the profiles, he ran his eye along their recent posts. Nothing very exciting. Photographs of day trips, notes on books they had been reading. A couple of comments about recent television programmes. None of them had mentioned their attendance at the evening class or the attack on Margaret, although it had been on the local news. Perhaps they had felt that it would have been in bad taste.

Disappointed, he sat back again. Apart from knowing a bit more about their lives, as in how many children and grandchildren they had and that they all enjoyed a visit to a stately home, he knew precious little about them. Helen, Moira and Diana. Ordinary women with ordinary names. Was it really possible that one of them was anything but ordinary? Could one of them have not only been involved in the murder of three children but carried out a particularly vicious attack on Margaret? Or could all three of them somehow be involved? They had all, by their own admission, been living in the town at the time of the murders. But then so had thousands of other people. As so often, he was in danger of letting his imagination run away with him. He stared down at the screen again, flicking between the images. Three kindly faces looked back at him.

He sighed. There was still Nicholas.

He typed in Nicholas's name and then stopped, fingers still raised. A memory, no, not a memory, more of a recognition, had just stirred. He sat perfectly still for a moment willing himself to identify it. It was no good. Whatever had just spiked his brain had melted away again. Never mind, it would come back. He peered more closely at the screen.

God, there were a lot of Nicholas Shaws. He scrolled quickly through them. There didn't seem to be any that related to the Nicholas Shaw that he was looking for though. They were either too young or too old, or lived in a different area of the country, or did a job that bore no relation to libraries. There were none that he could pin down. Several profiles also had no identifying picture and no personal information so while he couldn't count them in, he couldn't count them out either. Nicholas could easily be one of those.

He sat back and thought for a moment. It was possible of course that Nicholas didn't have a Facebook account. He didn't have one himself. But he wondered why Nicholas might not have one or, if he did, he posted nothing on it. Possibly it was because, like him, he was wary of social media. Perhaps he just liked to keep his private life exactly that. Private. There was nothing wrong with that. Annoying though, just at the present.

Carlos, unhooking his ears, looked up from his recipe book.

"Are you searching for those people again?"

Jeremy nodded.

"Yes, just checking their social media. Molly let me have access to Lilac Tree Lodge accounts."

"Found anything?"

"No, not really."

"What about that Margaret?"

"What about her?"

"Have you checked her out as well?"

Jeremy felt a sudden thrill of excitement. Margaret. Of course. It was obvious. Why hadn't he thought of it himself? As well as being a former journalist, Margaret was writing a book. If Lilac Tree Lodge used social media to promote themselves then presumably authors did too. Even though the book wasn't published yet, she would almost certainly have started posting about it. She might have written some kind of trailer, something that would give an indication of what she had found out. He caught his breath. She may even have written something that pointed in the direction of whoever it was that had attacked her. Hunching forward he tapped in Margaret's name.

CHAPTER NINETEEN

He was right. Scanning his eye quickly down her posts, Margaret had been using both Facebook and Instagram to promote not only the book that she was currently writing, but the next one she had planned which focused on the Victorian penchant for poisoning. No wonder she had been such an expert in class.

He glanced back at her Facebook profile. The picture was a good one, obviously taken by a professional and also obviously taken several years ago. He looked at it more closely. It was clearly Margaret. Just Margaret at her very best. Which, he guessed, was how it should be. After all, Margaret wanted people to buy her books and to some extent these days that meant selling herself as well. She'd said nothing about her marital status though, and she hadn't given her date of birth. He wasn't surprised. She was clearly promoting the public persona not the private individual, and there were a lot of nutters out there. He should know. He'd taught a few of them.

He scanned the few lines about her career. Working for one of the quality papers, she had clearly been a serious journalist in her day. She had also given her current occupation as author of true crime.

He flicked back again to her recent posts. The last one had been about her being so pleased to have been invited to deliver a series of lectures on local history. She had written about how much she was looking forward to the first in the series, and she had included the date and the venue. Not surprisingly, there had been nothing since although several people had asked how it had gone. But just below that had been some text about the golf course murders and her forthcoming book. He read over it several times. Margaret was very clever. There was just enough to pique interest without actually giving anything away. Each comment was a spicy little taster of what was to come and posed as a series of questions, to which surely the least curious person would want to know the answers. However, he quickly realised that there was nothing there that wasn't already in the public domain.

Glancing down at the top of the screen, he noticed for the first time something called 'friends'. He felt a sudden rush of hope. Possibly there would be something of interest there. He tapped the icon and stared in disbelief at the seemingly never-ending list of names that sprang up. There were hundreds of them. Surely that was a mistake. How many people had that many friends? He would think himself lucky if he could count a dozen and that included old school friends and former colleagues that he hadn't seen in years. He laid the tablet to one side and looked across at Carlos who had plugged his earphones in again. Leaning forward he gently tapped Carlos on the knee, who obligingly unplugged himself.

"Carlos, how many friends have you got on Facebook?"

"Dunno. Loads."

Jeremy smiled. Loads was a classic teenage response, along

with nothing and don't know. Loads could mean anything from five to five hundred.

"But how many?" he persisted.

"Hold on, I'll have a look."

Jeremy watched as Carlos tapped expertly at his phone.

"Three hundred and forty," said Carlos, looking up again.

"What?"

"Three hundred and forty," repeated Carlos patiently.

Jeremy looked astonished. How on earth did Carlos know so many people? As far as Jeremy was aware, Carlos had his mates at college, like Rubble, but they would amount to about seven or eight at most.

"Are they really, you know, friends? Like actual friends? I mean, do you know them?"

Carlos tipped his head to one side and smiled.

"Course not."

"Well how is it that they're your friends then?"

Jeremy felt confused. To him, a friend was somebody you knew. Somebody you had a shared past or interests with. Somebody with whom you maintained contact, even if you didn't see them regularly. They were people to whom you wrote birthday and Christmas cards. Or, to be more accurate, people to whom Molly wrote birthday and Christmas cards, passing them to him to sign before posting them. So who were these three hundred and forty people that Carlos had shared interests with? He wondered suddenly if he really wanted to find out. Was he about to plunge head first into some dark abyss that he would be better off not knowing about?

"It's just how it works," said Carlos.

"Is it?"

"People ask to be your friend and you can accept or not. But," he added, "if you want people to read your posts then it's better to have lots of friends."

"Right." Jeremy nodded. That made sense. There was no point in posting something if you didn't want people to read it. You might as well just talk to yourself. Also, it sounded innocent enough. Like modern-day diaries, except that you didn't keep the entries secret. And it had the added advantage that you presented yourself in the best light and simply edited out anything that you didn't like. It definitely had a certain simple attraction. He smiled slightly. There was a real danger that future generations would believe that twenty-first century people were all beautiful and led interesting, altruistic, fascinating lives. Still, it was, he supposed, a way of ensuring posterity. He knew that things posted on the internet didn't get burned or buried. They floated about in the ether forever. That was just the way the virtual world worked. Even if you deleted a post, somebody somewhere would have saved it. As a number of people had found to their cost. In many respects he didn't envy the youth of today. When he had been young, if you made a fool of yourself by getting off your face and being stupid the worst thing you had to do was go back and apologise. You didn't face the prospect of the whole sorry spectacle being broadcast across the globe. It made him shudder just to think of it.

"So if you don't know these people," he continued, "how do they actually know you? I mean..." He stopped. What did he mean? He'd thought that all this stuff was easy. He wasn't so sure now.

"People ask to be your friend because you might, like, be a friend of one of theirs," said Carlos. "A friend of a friend. Or they might have read something that you posted and liked it. So it sort of builds up. When I first had Facebook I just accepted everyone who asked."

Jeremy felt a desire to laugh. So there might be some person with, apparently, hundreds of friends who spent every night and day alone in a squalid little bedsit hunched over a laptop in tracksuit bottoms, eating microwaved ready meals and drinking cheap lager. Some person who, in reality, didn't have any friends at all. He felt suddenly ashamed of himself. Better that the lonely person in the squalid little bedsit had some virtual friends than no friends at all. Better to have some contact with the world, even if it was a virtual world, than no contact at all. And who was he, Jeremy, to scoff at that?

"And do you keep in contact with them all?" he asked.

Carlos shook his head.

"No. I hardly ever use Facebook. I just got it to see if I could find out anything about my dad. Like I said, it's really for old people."

Jeremy stood up and stretched. He wasn't offended by Carlos placing him in the category of old people. Carlos thought anybody over thirty was old, just as he had when he was Carlos's age. Anyway, he'd spent long enough on all this. The morning was practically gone, it was a lovely day out there and, now he knew how it worked, it seemed unlikely that he would get anything from Margaret's 'friends'. He cast a final glance at her profile and then peered down more closely. There was some kind of link embedded in the text. Margaret had a podcast.

CHAPTER TWENTY

Jeremy pushed open the door of the pub and looked around him. The room was already filling with weekend lunchtime drinkers, they'd be lucky to get a table. Noticing a free one in the far corner he moved quickly towards it. He turned as a voice behind him spoke.

"Well spotted, mate," said Mike. "Pint?"

Jeremy grinned and nodded. It had been a good idea to ring Mike. If the podcast contained anything of interest it would be better to have somebody to talk to about it, and four ears were better than two. Also, if he was honest, he only had a very vague notion of what a podcast was. He had an idea that they were some sort of recorded talks or interviews, but he'd never actually listened to one although Molly had told him more than once that he was missing out. He was beginning to think that she had a point. Anyway, there was no denying that a pint on a Saturday lunchtime was a thing of joy. And given the alacrity with which Mike had agreed to meet him, he suspected that it was a thought with which Mike thoroughly concurred.

"So what have you found?"

Mike placed the two pints on the table and sat down. He looked across expectantly.

Jeremy laid Molly's tablet between them.

"I had a look at Margaret's Facebook page. And found this."

He flicked open the cover of the tablet and turned it round to face Mike. He watched as Mike picked it up and ran his experienced police eye over the text, frowning as he did so.

"I'm guessing it's the podcast we're interested in?"

Jeremy nodded. "Yes. As you can see, in her posts she doesn't actually tell us anything that we don't already know about the golf course murders but she's clearly setting out her stall."

"Have you listened to it yet?"

"No. I thought it would be better if we listened together. Of course, it might not tell us anything."

"Only one way to find out."

Mike reached out and tapped the screen. Instinctively the two men leaned forward as Margaret's voice filtered out.

'Sally, Tommy and Ruth. The names of three very ordinary children...'

"Let's go to the most recent episode," said Mike. "We can listen to the earlier stuff later on."

He pressed pause and then opened episode seven which appeared to be the last one that Margaret had recorded. Ten minutes later the two men sat back and regarded each other. For several moments neither of them spoke.

"I wasn't expecting that," said Jeremy eventually. He wasn't quite sure what he had been expecting, but it wasn't that.

"She said that it had only recently come into the system," said Mike, speaking slowly as he turned the idea over. "She didn't say how or why but it may have been because of something quite trivial. It wouldn't be the first time. It has been known for criminals to be caught years after the event because of a DNA match. Remember Wearside Jack."

"Who?"

"Wearside Jack. He was the bloke who sent the hoax letters to the police searching for the Yorkshire Ripper. The letters were kept and, years later, they did a cold case review. A DNA trace was found on one of the hoaxer's envelopes which matched a set in the system."

"Blimey." Jeremy paused and took a mouthful of beer. "But if you're right, and I'm sure you are, why haven't the police done anything about it? I mean, surely, they would have been straight on it?"

Mike shrugged.

"Could be any number of reasons. The fact that they haven't gone public with anything doesn't mean there's nothing happening. There's always a lot goes on behind the scenes in any serious case, and there'll be a lot of checking and double-checking in this particular instance before any arrests or announcements are made. It's a case that still attracts interest even now. And remember Harvey. The police won't want to make that mistake again. And there'll be plenty to remind them if they get it wrong for a second time."

"Yes, I guess that's true. But if the police haven't said anything yet how do you think that Margaret knows about it?"

Mike smiled and took a sip of his pint.

"It's obvious. She's got a contact somewhere on the inside. Probably several."

Jeremy nodded. Again, Mike was almost certainly right. Margaret was a former journalist. She must have had contacts all over the place. That was how the press got the inside info on the stories that they ran. And police officers would be an obvious source. Given the kind of research that she was engaged in, as a true-crime author, she had probably kept up the acquaintances.

"It might be a civilian working in the system, but my bet is that it's a copper," continued Mike. "It usually is."

"Are they allowed? I mean isn't it against the rules or something?"

"Depends. Obviously police officers shouldn't be doing it for money. That's misconduct in a public office and you can go to prison for it. One of my own officers fell prey to the lure of easy money about ten years ago. High profile case, involved a member of Parliament. Anyway, he got eight months. Silly little sod didn't even hide his tracks very well. Once we started looking for the leak, it was obvious that it was him. But it must be admitted that sometimes journalists are very useful to the police and vice versa. Most forces have some kind of reciprocal arrangement with the press, official or otherwise."

"So you think it's a serving police officer then?" asked Jeremy. "I mean, someone who's in the middle of things now?"

Mike grinned.

"Not necessarily. Just because you've left the force, it doesn't mean that you don't know what's going on. Police are like a family, you never really leave. And they gossip as much as anyone else. More, some might say."

"Did you ever join that Facebook group that meets up at the golf club?"

"Yes, I meant to tell you. I went to one of their gatherings last week."

"Any good?"

"Actually, yes. I only went along for something to do but I enjoyed it more than I thought I would. Funny thing..." Mike grinned. "For some reason I hadn't expected to see any women there. I think I just thought it would be a load of old retired codgers like me. Anyway, one I got talking to, Tracey, she's left the force now but she does some part-time work on cold cases. I told her that we were interested in the golf course murders and she said that she would let me know if she came across anything."

They both looked up as a young man approached their table and pulled back a chair. Carlos sat down.

"Molly's in Marks and Spencer. I told her where you were. She's coming over when she's finished shopping."

"Do you want a drink, Carlos?" asked Mike.

Carlos looked at Jeremy who gave a faint shake of the head.

"A Coke, please."

They both watched as Mike threaded his way towards the bar.

"I was coming to find you anyway," said Carlos. "I had a call from Rubble. I thought you'd be interested."

"What is it?" While Rubble might not be the brightest star in the intellectual firmament, he had an uncanny knack of acting as a conduit for useful information. It had been Rubble that had got him the class register.

"Rubble heard it from one of the cleaners that works at his dad's hotel. She does cleaning at the hospital as well. It's that Margaret." Carlos paused for dramatic effect and leaned in, lowering his voice slightly. "She's come round. She's conscious again."

CHAPTER TWENTY-ONE

Jeremy pushed the car door shut, flicked the electronic key at it, and looked up at the building in front of him. What happened, he wondered, to the old cosy brick-built hospitals that had one entrance, flower-beds out the front, and nurses that didn't look like they were about to service your car? When did hospitals start looking like some sort of grim miniature urban housing estates? He glanced around him. There were buildings all over the place and signs and directions everywhere. Given that for most people hospitals weren't a destination of choice, it was hardly a welcoming or calming environment.

He watched as a small portly figure emerged from a side entrance and stood directly under a sign informing visitors that the hospital was a no-smoking environment. Fumbling in her uniform pocket, she drew out a packet of cigarettes and lighter. Jeremy smiled and pulled out his phone, peering down to check the scribbled note he had photographed was still there. Having finally been persuaded by Carlos to use his mobile to store information rather than stuffing his pockets with scraps of paper, he still didn't quite trust it.

Margaret was on Level Three, apparently, wherever that was. He hesitated. Now that he was here, he felt a strange reluctance to enter the building. In there was a world that he didn't really want to know and even visiting someone somehow drew you in. It was as if you became part of a club that you didn't want to join. A club with its own rules and ways of doing things that you had to learn, whether you liked it or not. And there was no denying, when it came to body counts, hospitals scored pretty highly. He wished, not for the first time today, that Mike was with him as they had initially planned. But it had been Molly who had pointed out that two men Margaret had met only once turning up at her bedside might seem a bit alarming, not to say threatening, even if they were bearing a get-well card. And, in spite of his casual jeans and trainers, Mike did still look alarmingly like a copper. So it had fallen to Jeremy.

It was Carlos who had prompted the idea. Passing him a booklet that he had been given by Rubble, he had said that he thought Jeremy would be interested in it. Jeremy had cast his eye over it, expecting it to be an account of some Edwardian gourmet dinner or suchlike that Rubble had stumbled across. Instead, he had found himself reading an account of the golf course murders.

"Where did Rubble get this from?"

"He was looking in the basement of his dad's hotel for any old menu cards. It's for a project that we're doing on our course and he just found it stuffed in a box with some other things. He brought it into college to show me. I told him that you were interested in those kids and that," he added.

Rubble again. It was astonishing. The boy was a positive magnet for attracting useful information. Perhaps, in spite of an unpromising exterior, Rubble was destined for great things. One of those people on the periphery of history who didn't actually do anything, but who just managed by some quirk of fate to be in the right place at the right time. Anything was possible, you only had to look at some of today's politicians to know that. And his parents were loaded, which always helped.

He leaned back against the car and felt in his inside jacket pocket. Drawing the booklet out he studied it again. He'd read it so many times by now that he almost knew it by heart, but he still found it gripping. Printed on fairly decent although not high quality paper, the booklet had been produced to accompany a talk held by the Townswomen's Guild at the Mistletoe Hotel fifteen years previously. Concentrating on major incidents that had affected the town, the main feature was a sizeable section on the golf course murders and included an interview with one of the murdered child's parents. He felt his throat constrict and for a moment his vision blurred as he re-read the words.

Suddenly, standing in this bleak hospital car park with ominous dark rain clouds starting to gather, it all felt very real. It wasn't just a story, not just a news sensation to be gossiped over in the supermarket or pub. It was something that had actually happened. Happened here, in the very town that he was living in, and it had resulted in very real and lasting consequences. The people who had suffered had been real people who had their real lives ruined. And in the case of the children, three very real young lives had been suddenly and brutally ended.

It was one of the fathers who had been interviewed and there was a photograph of him alongside the text, staring stiffly into the camera. He looked, thought Jeremy, just like every other man of that era. There was nothing special about him, nothing distinctive. He was just your average bloke, Mr Everyman who went to work week in, week out and did his best. The kind of decent man who worked hard all his life, enjoyed watching the football on a Saturday afternoon, and looked forward to a peaceful retirement in his later years. Day had probably succeeded predictable day, until some lunatic had come along and thrust a grubby great festering hand into the mix and altered everything forever. The most poignant thing about the photograph, thought Jeremy, was that the man was wearing a jacket and tie. He had dressed up to have his photograph taken.

Whoever had conducted the interview had been skilful. The father had described in heart-breaking detail the day his daughter Sally went missing. It was a bright and sunny morning which had started like any other. He had gone to work and left the family having breakfast. He had been his usual cheerful self with no notion that it was the last time he would see his wife, his son and his daughter all together.

Jeremy looked up from the booklet and stared out across the car park at two distant figures, heads bowed, beetling back towards their car. Had they just had a last time? He felt a sudden melancholic recognition that one day it would be the last time that he saw or spoke to Molly. Or Carlos. Or Aubrey and Vincent. He hoped to God that he wouldn't know it when the time arrived. Or if he did that he wouldn't be saying something banal like 'Anything good on the telly tonight?'

He looked back down at the booklet. It had been the school holidays and Sally had gone out playing with her friend. They often stayed out all day when the sun was shining and he had given her some money to buy a sausage roll and a packet of crisps. In those days, he said, they didn't think so much about nutritional content. It was enough that the children were fed. Anyway, Sally liked sausage rolls and crisps. Jeremy sighed at the normality of it all. There had probably been scenes such as these playing out in homes all over England every day that summer, his own included. But it was this home, this family, for which everything had imploded with such terrifying ferocity that nothing would ever be the same again.

When, the interviewer had asked, would Sally normally have arrived home? About five o'clock he had said, but that day there was no sign of her by the time he got home from work just after five thirty. At first he and his wife hadn't been too worried, but as the late afternoon wore on into early evening they had begun to feel concerned. He remembered going back and forth to the window to see if she was coming up the road. By six thirty their concern had turned into mild panic. They had only recently acquired a telephone but not all of their daughter's friends had one in their home and so he had put his coat on and called round at as many of their houses as he could think of because, surely, she was playing at one of them. Only to discover that Ruth, Sally's best friend, was also missing. After that they had called the police.

Although his memory had been clear up until the time that Sally went missing, the days, weeks, and months after her body had been discovered had, he said, blurred in his memory. They had become a shifting shapeless form that flitted in and out of his waking moments. He had, he knew, gone to identify Sally's body but he remembered nothing about it later. For which, he said, he was deeply grateful. When he tried to remember what he had done or where he had gone after that dreadful day, he had only sharp visual pinpricks of particular events or incidents. The day of the funeral, when it seemed that most of the town had turned out, had passed in a haze.

When trying to recall it later, he couldn't have told you what time it was held or even what day of the week, far less what hymns had been sung or who had been present at the service. In stark contrast, the day he had returned to work was etched as deeply as the day it happened. All his workmates had fallen silent as he walked through the factory gates and they had parted to make way for him. He had lifted his head and stared straight ahead, terrified of seeing the expressions of sympathy on their faces. Although his legs had felt weak, he had forced himself to keep walking, pushing his leaden feet forward. He had been afraid that he would cry.

His first instinct, he said, had been to move home. He had felt a great urge to get far away from the town where his life had fallen apart. He wanted to start somewhere new where he wouldn't be faced with daily reminders of what he had lost, but in the end he stayed. He had realised finally that it wouldn't make any difference. Wherever he went, his grief would go with him and to move would have taken him from Sally's last resting place. In those early years it was the only place he could find peace. Every Saturday morning he and his wife and son had driven to the churchyard and, after replacing the flowers, stared down at Sally's grave without speaking. After twenty minutes or so they had driven home again in silence. Later, he visited on his own.

He had eventually separated from his wife. Their son, unable to articulate his own sorrow at the loss of the sister to whom he had been close, spent most of his time at friends' houses so that he and his wife were more often than not alone together. Long evenings spent trying to think of something to say, each struggling to find ways to help the other, had been too much for them. Their combined grief had, in the end, proved too heavy a weight for them to carry. They had, without even really talking about it, made the decision to live apart and his son had gone to live with his mother.

Having lived with his parents until he had married, he had found himself on his own for the first time in his life. He had rented a small flat on the seafront. It had been all right. He got used to it. He taught himself to cook and he had the television for company, but he missed his garden. Jeremy closed his eyes for a moment. The evil bastard who had killed this man's child robbed him of everything. Even his garden. Of the arrest, conviction and later release, of Harvey he said very little. But surely, knowing that the real killer had never been caught, knowing that he was still out there, possibly still living in the same town, somebody who he could have passed on the street or sat next to on a bus, surely that must have made everything so much worse.

CHAPTER TWENTY-TWO

Jeremy carried his hot mug carefully across the room, weaving between the tables to a vacant one by the window. The hospital café was unexpectedly warm and cheerful, with people bustling about and a faint but pleasant smell of baking in the air. He settled back in his chair and took a sip of coffee. The earlier threat of heavy rain had materialised and it was chucking it down out there now. It was all right. He was in no hurry. He'd just sit here until it eased off a little. Anyway, he wanted a bit of time and space to think.

He was glad now that he'd come, despite his earlier reservations. The inside of the hospital was much less daunting than he'd feared and Margaret had, he thought, been pleased to see him, although that was probably more to do with being stuck in a bed all day with nobody in particular to talk to rather than any personal qualities of his own.

She had, however, quite definitely been interested in the booklet. After asking how she was and handing her the card that he and Mike had bought, he had passed it to her and watched as she read through it, head tilted slightly to one side and glasses perched on the end of her nose. Finally laying it to one side she had spoken in a soft low voice.

"The families of the children were the first people I checked out when I started the research for the book. Not that I thought they could tell me anything I didn't already know but I wanted to find out how they'd coped over the years. I wanted the book to be not just another true-crime account, but to explore how it affected lives long into the future. I found Tommy's parents fairly quickly, even though they'd moved. And Ruth's mother had stayed in the same house. I knew, I can't remember how, that Sally's mother had died some years ago, so I was looking for her father. But then I saw the piece in the local paper saying that he had died as well."

He nodded. He routinely read the local paper himself, because it was interesting. He'd read only recently that the gardener who he often saw during his walks in the park and had sometimes passed the time of day with, had died unexpectedly. Apparently, he had once been a very talented photographer whose pictures had sold all over the world. Jeremy had Googled him and been amazed. You would never have guessed that he had led such a fascinating life from his gentle manner and shy exterior. He had wondered what had brought him to such a quiet life as a parks gardener in a seaside town and wished that he'd known about his past before so that he could have asked him. That was the problem with death. It was so very final.

Margaret had continued, her voice gathering strength as she spoke.

"The sad thing was that the obituary had very little to say about him as a person. The whole focus was on him being the father of one of the golf course murder victims. A dismal way to be remembered, don't you think?"

Jeremy had nodded in agreement. Dismal indeed. To be remembered primarily for your relationship to a victim of a terrible murder was beyond sad. It was tragic. He had sat down on the hard plastic of the visitor's chair and drawn closer while he listened to Margaret talking.

"Of course, I had met them all before. I was one of the journalists who interviewed them at the time of the murders, and I was one of the few members of the press allowed to attend the funeral. I think it was because I was young and they trusted me. The funeral was a triple event. All three children. A dreadful day."

She had fallen silent as though visualising it, the image of it long ago and far away but no less horrific for that. As he watched her, it had suddenly occurred to Jeremy that the murderer might also have attended the funerals. He may not have been in the church but he could easily have been among the mourners lining the pavements outside. Just another townsman mingling with the crowd, watching, listening. Maybe even expressing sorrow along with the rest of the people gathered together. It was such a horrible thought that he had shoved it straight to the back of his mind before any unwelcome pictures could form.

"It's very kind of you to bring this in for me," Margaret continued. "I might try and trace the person who did the interview, if they're still around, and ask if I can include any of it in my book." She held the booklet out to him. "Did you want it back?"

He had shaken his head. He'd already ascertained that Rubble had said he could keep it and he'd made several copies. He had left not long after. She had obviously been tired and he had been conscious of a nurse hovering in the background. He had intended to ask her about the attack, but somehow it had seemed inappropriate. Neither had he asked her about the contents of the podcast, although initially he had intended to.

He had, however, said that he would visit again if she would like him to.

"Mind if I sit down?"

Jeremy looked up, startled. He had been miles away. The man spoke again.

"Sorry, am I disturbing you?"

Jeremy smiled.

"Hello Nicholas. What are you doing here? Are you visiting someone?"

And as he spoke, the recollection that had been swirling around somewhere at the back of his mind when he had been checking Facebook came into focus. Nicholas Shaw. And Shaw had been the name of the little girl Sally who had been murdered. The one whose father, David Shaw, had been interviewed.

CHAPTER TWENTY-THREE

Aubrey walked towards him, tail in the air. Jeremy leaned over and tickled his ear.

"Hello, mate, what have you been up to?"

Nothing, thought Aubrey. Just bored and waiting for someone to come home, if only to provide a lap to sit on. Vincent had gone off somewhere on his own this afternoon, and hard though it was to believe, there were only so many hours that a cat could sleep. Even next-door's dog had been indifferent to his deliberate staring through their kitchen windows. In fact, the idle sod, slumped in his basket, had barely opened an eye.

"Come on in, Nicholas."

Aubrey turned and saw a man of medium height with greying hair climbing out of Jeremy's car. He felt a flick of disappointment. He'd been looking forward to some Jeremy time. Molly was still at work and Carlos was round at Rubble's house helping him with some coursework, so it would have been just the two of them. He eyed the visitor dispassionately. He wasn't someone that he'd seen around here before. Like most cats, when faced with a new person or situation, the default position was to keep a distance and mistrust. It was an instinct that he'd always followed and it hadn't let him down yet. He watched the two men enter the house and then slipped round the back to the cat flap.

"Tea? Or something stronger?"

Jeremy paused, one hand on the kettle.

Nicholas smiled, a shy smile that softened his features. From the far corner of the kitchen, Aubrey felt himself relax slightly. So far, so good.

"I don't mind. Whatever's easier."

Jeremy grinned.

"Lager okay? Saves boiling the kettle."

Aubrey watched as Jeremy pulled two cans from the fridge and ripped off the tabs. He passed one to Nicholas and then led the way to the sitting room. He gestured towards the sofa.

"Sit yourself down." He paused and then continued. "A hospital coffee shop didn't seem like the right place to talk. That's if you want to," he added.

Aubrey sidled round the door and looked at the visitor. He wanted to talk all right, Aubrey could see that. He had that sort of strained, slightly pumped expression that people wore when they really wanted to get something off their chest but didn't quite know where to start. Like that time Carlos had been persuaded to bunk off college with some of his mates and go to a demonstration in London. Fearing that there would be live footage on the news and that he might be spotted, he'd told Molly and Jeremy what he'd done. Aubrey didn't really know what a demonstration was and he half-suspected that Carlos didn't really know either. He certainly didn't seem to have any sort of grasp on what he had actually been doing there.

But it had been all right. Molly and Jeremy hadn't seemed too concerned, although they had made him promise not to do it on a college day again. That was one of the things he loved about them. They never really got worked up. Not unless you did something dreadful, like tread muddy paw prints all over the clean sheets just after they'd been changed. He shivered slightly at the recollection. He'd rather eat his own tail than be ticked off by Molly again.

He jumped on to Jeremy's lap and stretched himself out along his knee, resisting the urge to dig his claws in. He didn't want to get chucked out for being annoying just yet, he wanted to hear what these two were going to talk about. From the tension in the atmosphere, he suspected that it was something interesting. Anyway, he didn't have anything else to do.

"Can I see the booklet?" asked Nicholas.

"No, I gave it to Margaret."

Nicholas looked disappointed.

"But I made some copies," Jeremy continued. "Hang on, I'll get you one."

Lifting Aubrey gently to the floor, he left the room. Aubrey and Nicholas looked at each other.

"Hello," said Nicholas. "What's your name?"

Aubrey tipped his head to one side and regarded him. It was weird. People often said that to animals. Poor bloke would have had heart failure if he'd answered him. He turned as Jeremy re-entered the room and handed Nicholas some sheets of paper.

"There you go."

He scooped Aubrey up again and sat back. Aubrey watched as Nicholas scanned the sheets and then, visibly shaken, laid them back down on the small coffee table.

"I didn't know about this. I've never seen it before. As far as I knew, after the first interviews, my father never spoke about it again. Not even to me or Mum. Lots of the big tabloids wanted to pay the families for their story, but they all refused. Not that it put the journalists off. They were more or less camped outside for days, they were the first thing we saw every morning. I used to think that they would never go away. And then one day they just disappeared. Mum drew back the curtains and there was nobody there. I think another big story must have broken because suddenly they were all gone. Like migrating birds."

Nicholas looked thoughtful. "Once they left, it was weird. It was like it had never happened. The waters closed over it. Everything was just the same, except that Sally wasn't there anymore. Even when I went back to school nobody said anything, not a word. I guess the teachers told all the kids not to mention it. I think they thought that they were being kind but it made it worse in a way. I mean, it wasn't like nobody knew about it. Half the town turned out for the funerals, to say nothing of all the television and newspaper coverage."

"I expect they thought that they were doing the right thing," said Jeremy. "Although I'm not sure that there is a right way."

Aubrey agreed. When Carlos's mother had been murdered, far from maintaining a tactful silence, the kids at Sir Frank's had talked of nothing else for weeks. It had made him a school celebrity, as if there were a kind of glamour in it. Everyone had suddenly wanted to be his friend. From being the outsider who had struggled to fit in, he had been catapulted on to centre stage as the kid whose mum got killed. And he had hated it, Aubrey knew. As if trying to come to terms with the fact that she was gone wasn't bad enough, he had to face a daily reminder every time he walked through the school gates.

Although he had said nothing to Molly and Jeremy, he had often cried himself to sleep and had once even thought about running away. He'd explained his plan to Aubrey one night after a particularly trying day at school when there'd been a fight over who was going to sit next to him in Maths. As plans went, Aubrey had thought it was pretty crap. It seemed to involve going to London and getting on a train to Scotland, wherever that was. It was only the realisation that he had no money to get to London, let alone Scotland, that had put paid to it. That and the fact that he couldn't take Aubrey with him.

"I can't begin to imagine what it was like," said Jeremy after a moment's pause, the compassion clear in his voice. "It must have been really tough for you."

Nicholas nodded. "It was at first. It's not the kind of thing that you're ever prepared for. There's no dress rehearsal for your sister being murdered. But after a while I got used to it. I suppose when you're young, you get used to pretty much anything. Mum and Dad didn't talk about it at home and nobody talked about it at school, so it became like something separate. Like a before and an after. So there was life with Sally and then life without Sally. Mum and Dad even put Sally's school photograph away. It used to sit with mine on the mantelpiece and they put them both away." He paused for a moment. "I guess I can understand it."

"Didn't you have anybody to talk to at all? What about the other families?"

"Tommy's parents moved away very soon after, I don't know where. I'm not sure what happened to Ruth's parents, but she was an only child so there were no siblings. I've got a feeling that they stayed in the town. In any event, it was just me," he added bleakly.

Aubrey felt a twitch of discomfort. He'd had siblings, a brother and a sister. The last time he had seen them they had been tiny little kittens, sheltering under a hedge against the rain while they waited for their mother to return. Eventually he had wandered off to find her and got lost. That was when Raj had found him. Locking up his shop late one night, he'd noticed him soaked and dazzled by passing car headlights. He'd picked him up and taken him indoors. He'd never seen his brother and sister again although sometimes he still dreamed about them, such vivid dreams that he could feel again the press of their fragile little bodies as they huddled together to keep warm. He hoped that they had been lucky like him and had found good homes, that they hadn't simply perished under the hedge.

"It looks like your parents thought about moving too," said Jeremy, nodding towards the booklet. "Do you think that it might have been better for you if they had?"

"Maybe. But I don't think so, not really. Don't forget, it was a massive story. One child murder would make the headlines, but three... like Dad said in the interview, it would only have followed us. My parents separated anyway. I think that they couldn't bear being together in that house. The whole atmosphere changed."

Nicholas paused and looked thoughtful. "It was always such a happy home before, we had really good birthdays and Christmases there." He smiled. "Dad used to put up paper chains. Do you remember those?"

Jeremy nodded. "I do. We used to make them at primary school. They used to come in little packets."

"But after Sally died," Nicholas continued, "it was like we were all tiptoeing around, almost as though we didn't belong there anymore. Perhaps we didn't. There were no more paper chains after that. We didn't even have Christmas dinner like we used to. That first year without Sally we went to a local hotel but Mum thought that people were talking about us so we went home again. We must have eaten something, but I don't remember what. Probably just whatever was in the fridge. That's the thing..."

Nicholas took a long slow breath. "Whoever did that to Sally not only took her life, but they took everything away from us as well. Everything."

Aubrey sat quietly. There had been a subtle change in the atmosphere. A gentle sadness had descended on the room and he curled in closer against Jeremy.

"Did your parents never talk about Sally at all?" asked Jeremy.

"No. Not once. Not that I can remember, anyway. Her name was never mentioned and her bedroom door was always kept closed. My parents didn't tell me not to open it, but it was just understood that it was sort of out of bounds. But I did go in there once. I'd got up in the night to use the bathroom and I just crossed the hall and opened the door. I hadn't meant to, I just did it. It was strange. I can't really explain it but there was a kind of absence about the room, even though it was just as she'd left it. Her bed was still unmade and the book that she'd been reading was on the bedside cabinet. It was a library book but clearly my parents never returned it. I opened her wardrobe door as well and all her clothes were still hanging there. You could have imagined that she'd just walked out but you knew, inside, that she wasn't coming back. She was gone."

CHAPTER TWENTY-FOUR

Aubrey felt a sudden jolt of memory. When his old mate, Mr Telling, had been murdered in their last neighbourhood, he had gone back to his house and slipped through the cat flap. And Nicholas was right. There was a real and distinct difference between a room or a house that was empty because the occupier was out, and a room or a house that was empty because the occupier would never return. He listened as Nicholas continued talking.

"Anyway, by the time my parents separated they'd more or less stopped saying anything at all to each other. I don't mean in a bad way. They didn't argue or anything. It was just like they had nothing to say. Not to me, not to each other, not to anyone. After Sally was murdered, it was like a great big iron shutter came clanging down. We were living in a council house, so I guess all they had to do was give notice. The local authority gave me and Mum a house on the new estate that had just been built but Dad had to fend for himself. I think single men weren't a priority then. Probably still aren't."

"Were things any better once you'd moved?" asked Jeremy.

Nicholas thought for a moment.

"I suppose they were really. It sort of marked the start of the new life. Everything was different, even my route to school, so we didn't have so many reminders." He smiled. "Funny thing, usually, when there's some kind of hiatus in a family, the kids go off the rails. I went the other way. I started working hard at school and stayed on for the sixth form. Mum was really thrilled when I got a place at university. So was Dad. First one in the family."

He paused. "Poor Mum, she passed away soon after I left home. Apparently she more or less just sat down and died. I found out after that she had heart problems. It was Dad who arranged her funeral, even though they weren't living together anymore. It was only when I went through his things after he died that I discovered they had never got divorced." He fell silent for a moment. "Perhaps it would have been too final."

Jeremy nodded. He could understand that. While they couldn't stay together, they probably felt they couldn't break that last bond. He ran his hand gently over Aubrey's head, taking comfort from feeling the soft fur between his fingers. Not for the first time recently, he reminded himself how fortunate he was.

"After that I only came back briefly in the holidays," Nicholas continued. "Just to see Dad and make sure he was all right. The rest of the time I stayed away, went travelling or stayed with friends. Once I camped in the Highlands for the summer. To be honest it was a relief. I loved both my parents very much, but after Sally died it always felt as though I had to be better than I was. It's difficult to explain, but I was terrified of letting them down, of disappointing them in some way. I always felt as though I had to make them proud of me, to make up for them losing Sally. Once I was at university I could just be myself. I could leave the past behind and be a new person. I never told any of my new friends what had happened."

"But you came back here to live?" Jeremy asked.

Nicholas nodded.

"When Dad died, I came back to arrange the funeral and to sort his things out. Dad had an older brother, Uncle Lionel, but there was no other family apart from me. There wasn't really very much to do anyway. Dad had organised and paid for a funeral plan for himself and he had carried on living in the flat by the seafront. He hadn't really changed anything, it was all much as it was when he first moved in. I contacted a couple of charities to take his furniture and other bits and pieces and made a few trips to the tip, and that was more or less it. My plan had been to stay just as long as necessary to tie everything up. But that's when I found all the newspaper cuttings. They were in an old suitcase under his bed, along with some other things."

"What other things?" asked Jeremy, his tone curious.

"Photographs of us all on holiday, a toast rack that I made at school in woodwork. But they were mostly things of Sally's. Her school reports, a little box that she used to collect beads in, some annuals. And underneath it all was her favourite doll."

He paused and swallowed before continuing. "It was found in the air raid shelter along with her body. There were some other toys down there too, I think. I can't remember what they were exactly, they must have belonged to Ruth. Anyway, this doll, it was one of those teenage ones, I can't remember what they were called. Sindy or Tressy or something. She used to make clothes for it with a toy sewing machine that she got one Christmas. The police must have given it back to Mum and Dad and he'd kept it all these years. It gave me a shock, but it was seeing the doll that made me start wanting to know what had really happened. There was something about it. Something about the essence of Sally. That doll was with her when she died."

Aubrey shifted to make himself more comfortable. He'd had some toys once. When Molly and Jeremy had first brought him home from Sunny Banks Rescue Centre they had placed a small plastic ball with bells in it and a little plush bear inside his new basket, for comfort, he supposed. And if he was honest, while he wasn't bothered about the plastic ball, he had held that little bear close those first few nights in his new home. He watched as Nicholas turned his hands over and studied the palms, stretching his fingers out while he thought.

"For years, I had put it all to the back of my mind. Compartmentalised it, I suppose," he said eventually. "But when I saw the doll, dressed in the smart little blue dress, it brought it all back to me. I actually remembered Sally sewing that dress. It was made from leftover fabric that Mum had used to make Sally a dress. Standing in Dad's bedroom, holding that doll, was the first time I felt anger. I mean real rage. Not just because of what had happened to Sally, but for all of us. For me and my parents. And for Ruth and Tommy's parents, too."

"Is that what made you decide to come back to the town to live?"

"Pretty much. Although even before Dad died, I had already started turning it over in my mind, letting it sort of swill around. I wanted to try to find out a bit more about what had happened. I had lots of half-images that I remembered, and I wanted to somehow piece them together."

"Did you see any of the newspapers and so on at the time?" asked Jeremy.

Nicholas shook his head.

"No. Mum and Dad wouldn't let me. They wouldn't let me watch the news either. I expect they thought that they were doing the right thing but, looking back, I'm not sure that it helped. Although..." He paused for a moment. "I'm not sure that anything would have helped, really. Anyway, the result was I was left with lots of impressions but no hard facts. Not even a timeline."

"So what do you remember? If you don't mind me asking." Nicholas smiled.

"No, I don't mind at all. I think that this is probably the first time I've ever really talked about it." He thought for a moment. "So, I remember what I was doing the day they found Sally, that's probably the clearest memory. I'd got up early and decided to search for her. I knew that the people in the town had put groups together and obviously the police were searching and I wanted to help. I knew that my parents wouldn't let me, so I slipped out the back. They were up, I don't think they went to bed all the time that she was missing, but they were sitting in the front room. I could hear them talking. I went over to the park and there were police there and police dogs. I remember the police dogs. There was one called Bruno and the handling officer let me stroke him and then he said that he had to take me home again. I don't remember much else about that day apart from later, looking out of the front-room window and seeing a squad car pull up outside our house and two officers get out. They both put their hats on before knocking at the door and then took them off when Mum opened it."

For a moment the two men sat in silence, the grim image far too real for comfort.

"Do you remember anything else?" asked Jeremy.

"Only odd bits, nothing joined up. It was like there bwas a before Sally and then an after Sally, but with a kind of no man's land in the middle. Anyway, when I saw the advert for the county librarian post, I decided to apply and thought that I'd let fate deal the hand. My own life had pretty much fallen apart, I'd split up with my wife, so really I was free to go wherever I chose. If I didn't get the job that would be the end of it." He paused. "But I did get it."

"Did you have a plan?" asked Jeremy.

"Only in a general sense. I did all the obvious things, like reading the newspaper reports and so on." He smiled. "Typical librarian, I started to make notes and index them. I went back to look at our old house as well. In fact, going back to the street where we used to live was one of the first things that I did."

"Was it very different?"

Nicholas thought for a moment.

"The houses were smaller than I remembered. I think that the council had sold most of them off. Some of them had little porches built on the front. It was last summer. The curtains weren't drawn and some of the windows were open so I could see that there were people at home. I half thought about knocking on the door and asking if I could see inside, but then I thought better of it."

"You could have just said that you used to live there," suggested Jeremy. "They probably would have let you in."

"I thought of that, perhaps telling them that it was a sort of trip down memory lane. But then they would probably ask when that was and once they knew that, then they might work out the rest of it. I mean, even now, people still talk about the golf course murders. It's never really gone away. But while I was outside, I could hear them laughing at something on the television, like a normal family. It felt wrong to be there. I didn't want to spoil their evening."

"Did you know about Harvey being released?"

"Yes. My father wrote and told me at the time. He sent me the news clipping. So I always knew that the real murderer was still out there."

Nicholas looked again at the booklet.

"Poor Dad. His whole world collapsed. Well, it did for all of us really but at least me and Mum had each other. He was on his own. When him and Mum separated, I used to go and visit him in his little flat at the weekends. He used to be so pleased to see me. And he tried so hard, cooking me sausages and chips and buying me comics. He even bought a little cassette player for me to play my tapes on."

His voice suddenly broke and he fell silent again. Instinctively Aubrey climbed down from Jeremy's knee and jumped up on to the sofa next to Nicholas. He laid one paw on his arm. Nicholas looked down and suddenly buried his face in Aubrey's fur. Aubrey kept perfectly still. He could feel the almost imperceptible shake of Nicholas's shoulders. At last Nicholas looked up, his face pale but composed.

"We used to have a cat. It was Sally's. She had it from when it was a kitten. It was called Scamp. A little orange and white one. It was really naughty, used to get up to all sorts of things, but we loved it."

Aubrey sat up, interested. He liked the sound of this Scamp.

"After Sally died, Scamp went missing. We never found her although we looked everywhere. Dad put posters up on lamp-posts asking people to look in their sheds and so on but we didn't see her again. We never got another one."

"Does Margaret..." Jeremy hesitated and then ploughed on. "Does Margaret know who you are?"

Nicholas shook his head.

"I don't think so, no. Shaw is a common enough name and I was only a boy at the time so she wouldn't have recognised me. But I knew who she was. I remembered her. My parents only spoke to a few journalists but she was one of them. I remember her interviewing them in our front room just after it happened."

"Did you know that she was the tutor on the local history course?"

Nicholas shook his head.

"No. That was complete coincidence. I joined the course pretty much for something to do and to learn a bit more about the town where I was born, I guess. It was only when she started to talk about the golf course murders and the book that she was writing that the penny dropped."

CHAPTER TWENTY-FIVE

For several moments the two men sat in silence. Jeremy spoke first.

"Will you tell Margaret who you are now?"

"Yes. I was summoning up the courage to visit her when I ran into you at the hospital. I thought a coffee would steady my nerves." He paused and then said, "I checked her out on social media."

"I guess you know that she's got a podcast then?"

Nicholas nodded.

"Have you listened to it yet?" Jeremy's tone was hesitant. He was, Aubrey could see, feeling his way.

"I have."

"So you know about the DNA?"

"Yes, but I'm not sure if it makes things better or worse."

"Better, surely?" Jeremy looked perplexed. "I mean DNA evidence is pretty conclusive these days."

"I suppose... well, when she told us in class about the book that she was writing, I could hardly believe my ears. I had barely started my research and here was somebody who had already done most of it. Finally, it looked as though the truth would come out. From what she said, she seemed fairly certain who was responsible. When I got home that night, the first thing I did was to Google her. I also found her Facebook account. And the podcast."

Jeremy took a mouthful of lager while he thought about it.

"I still don't see the problem," he said at last.

"Don't you? If the DNA has only just been discovered then it looks like he's still alive. I mean, I want to know what happened to my sister and why but..."

"But if he is still alive then he'll go to prison. He'll finally get what he deserves. Wouldn't you want that?"

"Of course. But think what that would mean."

"What?" Jeremy sounded puzzled. "What would it mean?"

"If he's still alive there'll be a trial. Everything would start all over again. The journalists. The news teams. The television coverage. It would only be a matter of time before somebody produced a documentary." Nicholas paused and swallowed. "This is the age of the internet. Somebody would be bound to find me. And I don't think I want to be found. I want to know what happened, sure, but I don't want my private life trampled all over."

"But, surely it would be quite difficult to track you down." Jeremy spoke slowly. "You don't do any social media or anything..."

"I've got accounts, I just don't post anything." Nicholas gave a rueful smile. "When I moved back here, I closed my old accounts and then opened new ones under an alias. I didn't want to post anything but I wanted access. These days people seem to live their lives on social media and there was a chance that I would pick something up. But I didn't want to do it under my real name. I thought it was unlikely that anybody would put two and two together, but I didn't want to take any chances. I didn't want to be outed. I read the piece about my father in the local paper, uncle Lionel sent it to me. It made me feel really sad, and quite angry in a way. As if the whole of my father's life was the sum of how his daughter died. I don't want that. I don't want to be remembered as the brother of a murdered child. But just using another name on social media wouldn't put a professional off the scent, particularly a determined professional. That was one of the reasons that I decided to tell Margaret who I am. There are all sorts of ways to find someone if you really want to and it would only be a matter of time. I decided that if anybody was going to interview me, then I wanted it to be Margaret, not some hack who didn't give a toss about any of us. At least Margaret was a serious journalist."

"Yes." Jeremy spoke slowly. "I see what you mean."

And he did see what Nicholas meant. Social media aside, it was very difficult to live in the twenty-first century without leaving a digital footprint somewhere. And once the story broke, the media would be like a rat up a drainpipe.

"There's something else as well," said Nicholas. "It's a bit of a strange coincidence really."

"What is it?"

Jeremy leaned forward, head on one side and one hand still clutching his now nearly empty can of lager.

"One of the women on the course..."

"What about her?"

"I knew her when I lived here before, when I was young."

Jeremy stared at Nicholas.

"When you say you knew her..."

"Not as a family friend or anything," said Nicholas. "I just knew who she was."

"So who is she?"

"Her husband was our family doctor. He used to play golf and sometimes me and my friends would go up to the club and offer to caddy for the members. It was a good way of earning a bit of pocket money. Anyway, his wife often used to pick him up and they would have a drink in the club bar. I used to see her in there."

"What? You were drinking in the golf club bar?"

Nicholas laughed.

"No. That was one of the other jobs that me and my mates used to do, gather up the empties and wash them. But the doctor's wife, she was quite a lot younger than him, I suppose that's why I remembered her. She always seemed different from the other wives somehow. Not so loud. A bit shy. And she was the only one who bothered to say thank you when we cleared their table."

"Do you think it's got any bearing on things?"

"I don't know. What I do know is that they came round to see us after it happened. They bought my mum some flowers and stayed for a cup of tea. I remember that he talked a lot. She didn't say very much."

Jeremy thought for a moment.

"It's odd then that she didn't say anything when we were all talking in the pub the other night. I mean, you would have thought that she might mention that she actually knew one of the families."

"I know. I waited for her to say something but she didn't. She obviously didn't know who I was."

"Perhaps she didn't remember your family?"

Even as he said it, Jeremy knew that it was unlikely. She was living in the town when the murders happened. She must have known that one of the victims was a patient of her husband's. And visiting the parents of a murdered child wasn't exactly an everyday occurrence. So why didn't she just say that her husband had been the Shaw family doctor?

Could he have somehow been involved? He certainly wouldn't be the first murdering doctor. But he had taken flowers and shared a pot of tea. Surely he wouldn't have done that if he'd played a part in the crime? He was just being kindly, and doctors did routinely pay home visits in those days. He was just concerned for the welfare of some of his patients who were suffering the most dreadful ordeal. What other reason could he have had for going there?

CHAPTER TWENTY-SIX

Aubrey jumped down from the sofa as the click-clack sound of the cat flap drifted through from the kitchen. Either they had an intruder or Vincent was home.

"All right, Vin?"

Vincent nodded.

"Good, mate. You?"

"Good."

He watched as Vincent strolled leisurely over to his food bowl, sniffed delicately and then turned away. Aubrey looked at him, concerned. He would have thought that Vincent would have been hungry by now, he'd been out for ages. He would have been, he knew. Food was never very far from his mind. An awful thought suddenly struck him.

Was Vincent double-bedding it? Was he living, and, therefore, dining, somewhere else as well? Some cats did, he knew. Gordon over the way had been living in a number of other houses. When his owner had pinned a note to his collar asking anyone who was feeding him to ring her, she had been inundated with calls. Gordon had thought it was funny, in fact he'd boasted about it.

Aubrey didn't think it was funny at all. He had always held the view that if somebody had the decency to pick you from the Big House and give you a new home, then the least you could do was be loyal. A number of cats didn't see eye to eye with him on that one though. Their view was that it was every cat for him or herself and free food was free food.

But not Vincent, surely? Not when Molly and Jeremy had been so good to him. Without them stepping in when his owners had disappeared, Vincent could still be in the Big House even to this day. But now he thought about it, second and third homes weren't something that they'd ever discussed. He'd just assumed that Vin was of the same mind as him. But what if he wasn't?

"Think I'll go and have a bit of a kip," said Vincent. He yawned and stretched, arching his sleek back. "Bit tired today."

Aubrey watched in surprise as Vincent headed to his cat dome under the radiator. They rarely used the expensive, fleece-lined cat domes that Molly had bought them, preferring instead the second shelf of the airing cupboard when they could hook the door open or one of the family beds upstairs. Empty cardboard boxes were good, too, although they usually got recycled before they had a chance to get their paws on them.

For a moment Aubrey watched as Vincent climbed in, curled in on himself and closed his eyes. Ah well, if Vincent fancied a nap it was better to leave him to it. He turned as Jeremy came into the kitchen carrying two empty lager cans which he tipped into the kitchen bin. Aubrey grinned. Molly would kill him if she caught him doing that. She was big on recycling and so was Carlos. Too much so, Aubrey sometimes thought. All manner of interesting things went into the recycling bin before he'd had a chance to investigate them properly. While he routinely went through the kitchen bin, jumping on the pedal to open it, he steered clear of the big green recycling one after hearing what had happened to Titan.

"Just going to run Nicholas home," said Jeremy, reaching into his pocket for his car keys. "See you later."

That was one of the many things that he loved about being in this family, he thought. In fact, it was a bit like when he'd lived with his first owner. During those long evenings sitting in the back of his failing shop, Raj had always talked to him while he sipped at his whisky, talked to him properly, as an equal, not stupid animal talk that even animals didn't understand. He turned back to Vincent. He was out like a light. Perhaps he'd get a bit of fresh air while Vincent was asleep.

He trod lightly along the road, keeping to the hedges in case he attracted the wrong sort of attention. This was a nice neighbourhood but cat-haters got in everywhere and the mere sight of a feline seemed to make some of them start foaming at the mouth. In fact, it was one of the few advantages he could see to being a dog. Dog-haters didn't usually start laying into one as soon as they clapped eyes on it, on the basis that it was likely to be an unequal competition. Cats, on the other hand, although more than capable of holding their own against another cat, had more or less no chance when confronted with a surprise attack by a human. They could lash out and inflict a few superficial wounds, but that was about it. It was often game over before they could get started. Anyway, when out and about it was always better to keep a low profile.

But the fear of cat-haters aside, he was glad he was out of doors. He'd been tempted to stay in and wait for Carlos or Molly to come home but he was feeling bothered about Vincent and a good walk would clear his head. Dusk was just starting to fall and it was a time of day that he particularly liked. There was something about the shadowy stillness of it that appealed to him. In the houses around him the lights were starting to come on and people were drawing their curtains.

Aubrey sniffed the air. It was very calm out this evening, the earlier rain had washed the pavements and he felt at peace with the world. He padded slowly along, enjoying the feeling of freedom and knowing that he could come and go as he pleased. Although he'd lived with Molly and Jeremy for some time now, he still didn't take it for granted. The time he'd spent in the Big House after Raj had died, when the possibility of getting out for a stroll had been roughly nil, had left its mark.

He stopped suddenly as a small sound tickled his ears. He listened harder. There it was again. He turned his head but there was nothing there. He started to move forward and then stopped again as the noise, tiny but insistent, continued. He stepped back and raised his head. There, perched on the bonnet of a parked car, sat Clara.

"Clara, what are you doing up there?"

Clara looked down on him, her pretty face screwed up in distress. She opened her mouth to speak but nothing came out. Aubrey moved forward.

"Come on, let's get you down."

He moved round to the front of the car and reached his paws upwards. He wouldn't be able to lift her down but at least he could be there to catch her. He wrapped his front paws round her as she slithered down the bonnet and then gently guided her to the ground.

"Home for you, I think."

He looked around him. He'd only been there once but he was sure he could remember where Clara lived. It wasn't far anyway. He'd see her safely in and then he'd probably go home himself. Vincent would be awake by then and they could plan what they were going to do for the rest of the evening. Together they trotted silently along the road, him keeping to the outside and Clara tucked in next to him. He glanced down at her. She was such a trusting little creature.

In fact, she was a bit like Moses, the tiny little cat that had been part of their gang at the old house. Moses had been remarkably dim, barely able to hold an idea in his furry little head for more than two seconds at a time, but he had been unwaveringly loyal and he had the courage of a lion. When they'd had their big bundle up at The Laurels with their enemy cats from the neighbouring manor, Moses had more than played his part. The sight of Moses hanging on to the back of a huge white enemy cat twice his size had stayed with them all. Aubrey sighed. Much as he liked this neighbourhood with the beach and all the interesting things washed up from the sea, to say nothing of the little rock pools into which he could gaze for hours, he still missed their old home occasionally.

He nudged Clara gently as they reached the end of the road and turned into the avenue in which she lived. Clara, sensing that safety was close, picked up her step and ran lightly ahead. Aubrey smiled. Clara might be losing it, but she could still scent home when it was near.

He followed her along the front path and round the side of the house. He'd see her safely through the cat flap and then set off again. He could do with a bite to eat now, he was getting a bit peckish. He pulled up short. There, sitting round a table were grouped three women.

Helen, Moira and Diana sat at the patio table, their faces lit by three fat scented candles planted in the middle. In front of each of them stood a glass of wine.

"Cheers," said Moira, raising her glass.

The other two smiled, and raised their glasses in return. Aubrey watched them, interested. He'd never understood why they did that lifting their glasses thing. He'd asked Vincent and he didn't know either.

"Well," said Helen. "That's another stately home ticked off the list. We'll be running out of them at this rate."

Her friends smiled in response.

Moira picked up her glass and swilled the wine round, watching the gleam as it caught the light of the candle.

"What did you think of the local history lecture this week?" she asked.

"He was okay," said Diana, pushing her glasses further up her nose. "He seems to know his stuff at any rate. But I didn't think that he was as interesting as Margaret. Poor Margaret," she added. "It was such a dreadful thing to happen. I can still hardly believe it."

"Talking of whom," said Moira. "Has anyone got any news?"

Aubrey slipped further into the cover of the shadows. Margaret was the woman that had been attacked. She was the one that Jeremy was all bothered about. He felt a soft shape settle beside him. Clara. So she hadn't gone indoors as he had thought but it was all right, as long as she didn't wander off again. He laid a paw gently on her tail to keep her close.

"I don't think the police are any further forward," said Diana. "At least, not that I've heard. It's odd though, she wasn't robbed or anything. It said in the paper that nothing was taken. There must have been some other reason."

"I wonder what, though?" said Moira. "People don't just get randomly attacked like that. Not in this town anyway."

That's where you're wrong, thought Aubrey. He and Vincent had witnessed an attack only last week on one of the homeless people who slept in the park. Some youths, making their drunken way home from the town's only nightclub, had thought it was funny to kick him awake. They hadn't taken anything, but only, thought Aubrey, because the poor soul had nothing to take. He and Vincent had stayed with him that night, if only to keep him warm.

He looked more closely at the women. Smart, comfortable, obviously well fed, he doubted that any of them would ever be reduced to sleeping in the park. In fact, he doubted that any of them were even aware that anybody did sleep in the park.

"Well, it will probably delay her book coming out," said Helen. "I think she said that it was due to be published in the summer."

"You don't suppose," Moira spoke slowly, "that it might be connected in some way?"

Diana sat up straighter and tipped her head to one side slightly while she thought for a moment.

"What, she was attacked to stop her publishing? It could be, I suppose. She did say that lots of people would be shocked. A bit drastic though."

"I agree that it's possible," said Helen. "But it does seem rather far-fetched."

"I guess you're right," said Moira. "It was just a thought. Although I suspect that there's probably quite a few people still living here who wouldn't want reminding of that time."

"It certainly didn't do our reputation much good," agreed Diana. "Even now, people associate the name of the town with the murders. An estate agent that I know told me that it took years for sales to pick up. And the tourist trade definitely suffered, a couple of the smaller hotels went out of business. If she's really unearthed something, the whole thing might blow up again."

"It might," said Moira. "But really, it was all years ago. Would that be a good enough reason to try to stop the book?"

It might, thought Aubrey. One person sitting right here at this table might have a very good reason to stop Margaret talking. He thought back to the day she had been burning something in the garden. She had been talking to Clara, her voice thickening with the whisky she was drinking, and amongst the mutterings, much of which he hadn't understood, there had definitely been mention of Margaret and her book. Something that she was afraid of. He inched forward and looked at the woman more closely. Was it really possible? It was difficult to tell from her face. She looked like such an ordinary person. There was no sign of strain or tension. Dressed in a light jacket, sensible skirt and comfortable shoes, she was practically indistinguishable from her friends.

"It was so long ago." Diana took a sip of wine. "And yet, in a way, it seems like yesterday."

Moira nodded in agreement.

"It was a horrible time. Everybody was under suspicion. Do you remember? Everybody was looking at everybody else. I didn't know anybody who wasn't questioned. Any man, I mean. I know it sounds awful but I felt such a relief when they arrested Harvey."

"I think we all did, really," said Diana. "Poor Harvey. He was such a gentle soul."

"Well, at the time we all just wanted it to stop," said Moira. "And to be fair, after they arrested Harvey it did stop."

For a moment the three women sat in silence.

"The boy, Tommy..." said Diana eventually.

"What about him?" asked Helen.

"Do you remember him?"

"Vaguely." Helen thought for a moment. "Small fair-haired lad. Bit of a cheeky grin. He used to deliver our newspapers."

"Yes, he used to deliver ours too. Well, I know that one shouldn't speak ill of the dead and all that, but he really was a rather horrid little boy. Always poking his nose into things. I remember I had to tell him off once for looking through our windows."

Maybe he had poked his nose in once too often, thought Aubrey.

CHAPTER TWENTY-SEVEN

She stared out at the disappearing tail-lights of the taxi carrying her friends home and raised her hand in a farewell wave. She had been very tempted to cry off the stately home visit, even though she had been looking forward to it for some time, but she was glad now that she hadn't. It had been all right. Everything had been just as usual, even to them having a glass of wine together when they got off the coach.

They habitually took it in turns to host the drinks after a day out and this time it had been hers. They had been busy all day, absorbing the sights and sounds of the stately home, pointing out things in the guide book, having tea and cakes in the little café, and admiring the grounds, so they hadn't really talked about recent events but she had known the discussion would turn to Margaret once they sat down with a glass of wine. It would have been odd if it hadn't.

She walked back through to the garden and began collecting the empty glasses, holding them against her chest for a moment as she stared down across the shadowy lawn. It was dark now, the only light coming from neighbouring houses. There was a safety in darkness, she thought. She had been afraid of the dark as a child but when she had been married to Raymond one of her few comforts had been to sit in the garden at night. When the children were in bed and he had disappeared to his study claiming that he had work to do, she had often filled a large glass of wine and crept out, usually sitting on the children's swing.

Rocking gently to and fro she would let the wine work its magic and dream of the girl she used to be, wondering how her life would have been if she had married Brian. She wouldn't have the big house, or the smart car and wardrobe full of lovely clothes. But she would have the heart of a good man and that, as she knew now, was worth more than everything else put together.

She put the glasses back on the table and sat down, running the conversation with her friends through her mind again. She had said all the right things, she was sure. She'd asked predictable questions, showed just enough interest, and generally been completely normal. She had said nothing that would arouse any suspicion among the group. And why should they suspect her? She was one of them. They would never guess her to be anything other than the respectable widow of a local doctor, which in many respects she was. At least as far as outward appearances were concerned.

Really, today had been much easier than she had expected. Years of living with Raymond had made her expert in living a lie. She had been playing a part for years. It was almost second nature. All in all, she reassured herself, it had been okay. She had been ready for it. What she hadn't been ready for was seeing Nicholas Shaw again.

She hadn't recognised him the first time. Why would she? He had simply been another middle-aged man in the class like Jeremy and Mike. It was only when they were sitting in the pub together that the shock of recognition had hit her. There was something about the turn of the head, the way of half-smiling and the crinkling of the extraordinarily blue eyes.

He had been the boy that collected the glasses at the golf club bar. The boy whose sister had been murdered. He had been there the day that she and Raymond had visited his bereaved parents. He had hovered in the background, clearly unsure whether he should remain in the room or leave the adults to it and in the end he had slipped quietly out of the door and upstairs, presumably to his bedroom where he had stayed until they had left.

Her mind ran instinctively back to that day. It had been scorching, the temperature rising with each passing hour. Normally there would have been holidaymakers thronging the streets, but that day the town had been oppressively silent. There was very little traffic on the roads. It was as if everybody had quietly closed their front doors and retreated inside.

In her imagination, even the birds had stopped singing. She had been wearing a blue-and-white-striped cotton summer dress that felt cool against the heat of the day and her sandals felt light on her bare feet. After that day she had never worn that outfit again. The bodies of Sally and Ruth had been discovered the day before and people had been reeling from shock. The horror of discovering Tommy's body was yet to come.

It had been Raymond who had suggested visiting Sally's parents. Much as she felt for them, it had never occurred to her. When she had demurred, concerned that they would surely want to be left to deal with their dreadful loss in private, he had insisted. It was, he had said, his duty as their doctor to make sure that they were coping, to offer any help if it were needed and in the end she had been left with no choice but to go with him. They had sat stiffly in that hot little sitting room, the sun beating down outside, the scent of the flowers that Raymond had bought sweet and sickly.

She had listened in disbelief to his offers to help clear Sally's things if they would like him to. If they felt that it would be too much, he would be glad to take on the task for them. The parents had refused, sweetly, graciously. They weren't ready yet, they had said, but thanked him for his kind offer. They had left shortly after and he had driven away in stony-faced silence, his eyes hard and his mouth set. When they reached home he had gone straight to his study.

It had been, surely, the worst day of her life. Worse even than discovering Raymond's diary and photographs. She had known, sitting in that neat little room, balancing the matching cup and saucer on her lap – the cup and saucer from the set that surely the family didn't use other than on special occasions – that he had been involved in the murder of the two girls.

Why else would he take such an interest in people that he would have considered insignificant at the best of times? It was, she had realised with a sickening plummeting of her stomach, because he wanted access to anything of Sally's that might give him away. She was sure of it. He didn't have the same opportunity with the parents of Ruth or Tommy, he wasn't their family doctor, but he could at least try with Sally.

She pulled herself back to the present and looked around. The night air was cool and refreshing and she felt reluctant to go back indoors. The scent of spring flowers mingled with the scent of the perfume that Jack had bought her for her last birthday and she breathed it in.

It was a stronger perfume than she would normally have worn but she had grown to like it, it had a slightly heady aroma that made her feel young again. She picked up the wine bottle. There was still a bit left and she poured it into the nearest glass. She wasn't sure whose glass it had been but in the great scheme of things the danger of catching some germ or other from one of her friends was the least of her problems. She drank the wine in one gulp and then dropped her head into her hands.

She wasn't sure how much longer she could keep this up but she didn't have any choice. Margaret was still alive. She had to hope and pray she couldn't identify her. Come what may, she would have to hold her nerve. Not just for herself, but for Jack and Anna.

Aubrey watched as she raised her head and brushed her hair back from her face. It had turned into an unexpectedly interesting evening. They said that curiosity killed the cat. But it hadn't killed him. Yet.

CHAPTER TWENTY-EIGHT

Jeremy arrived first. He unbuckled his seat belt but remained where he was. The course looked particularly enticing today, it was fine and bright, perfect for a round of golf. He half-wished that he'd brought his clubs with him, he might have tempted the other two to a game. But perhaps not. Today was about more serious matters.

He glanced in his rear-view mirror at the sound of tyres crunching across the gravel and watched as Mike pulled up, with Nicholas just behind him. He got out of his car reluctantly. He didn't really want to do this, and he suspected that Mike didn't either, but both had felt that they had no choice. Not if they wanted to be supportive of Nicholas. Which they had agreed that they did.

"Are you all right, Nicholas?" asked Jeremy as he walked over to meet him.

"I'm fine," said Nicholas. "Thank you for coming today. I guess I could have done it on my own but..."

Mike exchanged a look with Jeremy. Following Jeremy's phone call to update him on the Nicholas development, it had been Mike's idea that the three of them should meet for a drink.

What they hadn't expected was that Nicholas would suggest a visit to the golf club.

"No need to thank us," said Mike. "We understand, don't we, Jeremy?"

Jeremy nodded. He did understand, in a way. Nicholas hadn't actually used the words acceptance or closure, but he suspected that was sort of what he was looking for. Part of that process was acknowledging the place where his sister had actually died. It was the same instinct that prompted people to tie bunches of flowers around lamp-posts at the sites of fatal accidents.

He looked at his new friend. He looked older today, his attractively boyish look wiped away and his face white and strained. His eyes were vivid blue against the paleness of his complexion. What must it have been like, Jeremy wondered, to have lived with the knowledge and pain of his sister's death all these years without ever really telling anyone about it?

Any death of a loved one was bad enough, but most people had at least one or two people to share the grief with. Nicholas apparently had nobody. And for it to have occurred in such a violent and shocking manner must be absolutely dreadful. And then to not feel able to talk about it, not be able to acknowledge it openly... it made it seem like a shameful secret, something to hide away.

It was, he suspected, a pattern that had been set by Nicholas's parents. Theirs had been the behaviour of a generation that didn't talk about their problems, that equated any show of emotion with weakness. They had a fear of somehow being exposed, of being found wanting in some way. Theirs had been a conspiracy of silence, and Nicholas had been too young to do anything other than go along with it. Over time, it had probably become a habit that was as familiar as putting on a comfortable old overcoat, a safety net against reality. But even comfortable old overcoats wear out eventually.

Nicholas smiled, a faint half-smile that held little joy.

"I know that it must probably seem a bit weird to you, but suddenly I just felt that it was something I had to do. That neglecting it all these years was somehow a denial of her." He shrugged. "I'm not sure that makes sense."

"We all deal with things differently," said Mike, gravely. "There's no right or wrong way in these matters. You must do what feels right for you."

Jeremy looked at him gratefully. There spoke the reassuring voice of the experienced copper. How many people over the years, he wondered, had taken comfort from it? He'd heard of the death knock, the practice of journalists knocking on the door of the bereaved to get a story, but policemen also had to do something similar. Except that theirs was the totally unenviable task not of seeking a reaction but of actually breaking the bad news. Did they get any training for it, he wondered? And if they did, would there really be any point? What could prepare you for shattering somebody's life in a few seconds? One thing was for sure though, the sight of a police officer walking up your garden path never augured good news. It wasn't ever like they were calling round to wish you a happy birthday.

"It's odd to think that I used to come here all the time." Nicholas's voice was low, hardly more than a murmur. Jeremy moved forward slightly to catch his words. "What with the caddying and collecting the glasses in the bar and so on. I knew the whole place really well. But after Sally died, I never came back. I couldn't. I never asked, but I'm fairly sure that my parents didn't come here either. We used to visit her grave regularly, but the golf course was never mentioned."

He glanced around him, his bright blue eyes taking in their

surroundings. "It's exactly how I've always remembered it. It doesn't look as though it's changed much."

"I don't think it has," said Mike. "I Googled some old pictures of the course last night and compared them to the present day. I had a look on Google Earth, too. The club opened in 1922 and apart from a small extension at the back it doesn't seem to have been altered since. The wasteland is still there, too. It hasn't been built on or anything."

Would it have made a difference, thought Jeremy, if it had been? He thought, on balance, it might. His old school had been constructed in the 1950s and then demolished to make way for a housing estate in the 1990s. He had found himself near the site a few years ago, driving back from a meeting on a bright summer's day, and on a whim he had gone to look at it.

Walking around among the neat little suburban houses, he had found himself disorientated. Where had the tennis courts and the science labs been sited? The old gym wall behind which he had tried smoking with a few friends was really difficult to locate, too. It had made him feel sad and in a strange way a little lonely. Afterwards he wished he hadn't gone.

However, today, unlike his feelings about his old school, he wished that the wasteland adjoining the golf course *had* been sold for development. It would have been so much better if it had been completely bulldozed, flattened beyond recognition. That the charnel house in which the girls had died had been filled in and built over.

The three men made their way across the course towards the eastern edge. In the distance, the golfers played on. Little Lowry figures silhouetted against the skyline, oblivious to the sad procession passing by, Jeremy paused and watched them for a moment. Some of them probably hadn't been born when the murders had happened. They may not even have heard of them. But if Margaret really had discovered the truth then the town would be all over the news once again and, inevitably, the golf course would be at the centre of it.

Any thoughts of escaping to the course for a quiet game of golf would be put on hold until the story blew over. And if there was a new trial, that could take some months. Maybe even years, given the current backlog in the court system.

Catching up with the other two, he joined them as they reached the wasteland. Around them the weeds and shrubs stood tall and strong, healthily defiant against the neglect of decades. Nicholas, walking slightly ahead, stopped and looked about him. He turned to his friends.

"It could be anywhere."

Jeremy nodded and cast an eye across the terrain.

"We're looking for some kind of brick or concrete entrance. They were built underground and had steps leading down. There was one in the grounds of my school," he added.

For several moments the three men strode about, each scuffing at the undergrowth with their feet in an effort to locate the entrance to the shelter. Above their heads, rooks circled, their black plumage stark against the blue sky, their raucous cawing resonating in the still air. Jeremy shivered slightly. This wasn't a peaceful place. It carried the stench of death. No wonder nobody wanted to build here.

"Here," said Mike, suddenly. "It's here."

Jeremy walked slowly towards him and looked at the entrance. It was almost exactly the same as the one in his school fields. Except that air raid shelter had been a place where teenaged boys had larked about, revelling in their youth. They had been confident and loud, with the whole world before them. In his memory it had always been the summer holidays.

How different to where they stood now. There was no confident, happy loudness here. No ghosts of boys larking about, pushing and shoving each other in teenaged exuberance. This was a quietly menacing place, where two little girls had met a violent death. Not for the first time, Jeremy wondered how the girls had been enticed down there. Perhaps they hadn't been. Perhaps they had been using it as a kind of den and the murderer had found them there. Perhaps he had been watching them for days.

Behind him he heard Nicholas clear his throat.

"Come on then," said Mike. Without waiting for a response, he led the way down.

Inside the shelter the air was surprisingly fresh. There must, thought Jeremy, be air vents somewhere. There was just enough light from the entrance to see by. He looked around him. Strewn about on the floor were several empty beer cans and an empty cigarette packet. In one corner, a broken canvas chair was collapsed on its side like a crumpled spider. Next to it lay a plastic cassette, its tape spooling out in a long shiny ribbon.

He leaned over and read the label. A band from about thirty years ago. So somebody had been down here since the murders, in spite of the grisly associations. Or perhaps because of it. There were some very odd people about. He straightened up and stood silently as Nicholas walked the length of the shelter, reaching out and touching the wall, laying the palm of one hand flat against the brick.

Jeremy glanced across at Mike who was staring studiously at the floor. He felt a sudden urge to get out, to run for the entrance and push his way up into the clean bright spring sunshine. To get away from this dreadful place. As if reading his mind, Nicholas spoke quietly, his face sombre.

"Let's go."

Jeremy pushed the back door open. The comforting smell of homemade chilli hung in the air and the kitchen looked friendly and welcoming after the claustrophobic gloominess of the air raid shelter. It had been a good idea to ask Carlos to cook something for them. It was just what they needed. Something normal and familiar to ground them in the here and now. He ushered his friends towards the table and waved them to sit down. Carlos turned from the hob and smiled at them.

"Nearly done," he said. He hesitated for a second. "How did it go?"

Jeremy and Mike turned to Nicholas. It was for him to say how he thought it had gone. While for them it had been a miserable experience and one which neither of them would be keen to repeat, it hadn't been traumatising. But how Nicholas had felt was difficult to tell. Once they'd left the air raid shelter, Nicholas had said very little, other than to accept Jeremy's invitation to lunch.

Nicholas looked at his two new friends. He hadn't really socialised much since he had taken up his new post, not unless you counted the odd leaving do. It felt good to be sitting here. It felt, in a strange way, as though he'd opened a new chapter. A good chapter. Being inside the air raid shelter had initially been even worse than he had imagined and he had been tempted to make a bolt for it, to run back up the steps and to keep running. He had pressed his lips tightly together, afraid to breathe in the air, frightened that it would cling to his clothing and soak through to his skin and that he would never be able to rinse himself of it. His heart had hammered so loudly that he was sure Jeremy and Mike could see it throbbing against his chest.

For several seconds, he had stood perfectly still, holding himself tense, and then he felt himself relax, a physical calming of the body that slowly trickled through him. Sally was no more here than she had been in her bedroom that night he had opened the door. Wherever she was, it wasn't here. He had moved forward and touched the walls, run his eye from ceiling to floor. It was just a brick building. That was all.

When they had re-emerged, he felt it had been a cleansing experience. The air raid shelter and the dreadful deed that had been committed there was no longer lodged in the dark recesses of his mind. It was no longer something that he had to hide for fear it would burst out and overwhelm him. For the first time since that terrible day that her body had been discovered, he was able to recall all the good things about Sally's life, without the memories being tainted by the dreadful ending of it. There was a kind of freedom in it.

He looked across at Carlos, noting the anxiety in the solemn dark eyes. He knew about Carlos's mother, Jeremy had told him. How strange that of the four people in the same room, two of them should have experienced the murder of a loved one.

"It was all right really." He gave Carlos a reassuring smile. "I'd imagined all sorts of things but, do you know, it was just a building. That was all. Just a building."

He watched as Carlos's shoulders relaxed as he turned back to the simmering pot and began ladling out large portions of chilli into the waiting bowls.

CHAPTER TWENTY-NINE

Aubrey opened one eye as the bedroom door opened and Carlos came in. He relaxed back into the warmth. It was all right, he didn't need to shift himself. Unlike Molly and Jeremy, Carlos didn't mind him being stretched out across his duvet. In fact, he positively encouraged it. More often than not Aubrey spent at least part of the night tucked in alongside him. From downstairs he could hear the comforting murmur of voices as Jeremy, Mike and Nicholas finished their coffee. He gave a contented sigh. Vincent was asleep in the airing cupboard and Molly would probably be home soon from the morning shift. All was well with the world.

He watched Carlos settle himself in front of his laptop and switch it on. Within seconds Teddy's pretty face appeared on the screen, smiling the little dimpling smile that always made a faint red flush creep up Carlos's neck.

"Carlos, I've been waiting for you to call."

"Sorry, I'm a bit late. I was making lunch for Jeremy and his friends. Chilli," he added.

"Was it all right?"

Carlos nodded.

"I think so. They ate it, anyway."

They did more than eat it, Aubrey thought. They'd scraped their plates clean and then all three of them had gone back for seconds. Just as well Molly wasn't keen on chilli. They'd finished the whole lot.

"They've been out looking at that murder place," Carlos continued. "Like, the place where those children got killed, the place where it actually happened."

"The air raid shelter?"

Carlos nodded.

"I asked my dad about those," Teddy continued. "He said that in the war, when there was a bombing raid on, people used to go down to the shelters for safety. Sometimes, they used to sing to keep their spirits up."

Bit tough if you didn't like singing, thought Aubrey. It must have been bad enough having high explosive bombs chucked at you but imagine being stuck down there with, say, Colin, their milkman. A small, ruddy man with thinning hair, Colin often whistled and sang to himself as he delivered the milk. The whistling wasn't so bad, but the singing... He and Vincent had heard better noises coming from the donkey in the field by the railway station.

"Anyway," said Carlos, "they're back now."

Teddy leaned in closer to the screen, her eyes opening wider.

"What did they say about it?"

"Nothing really. Nicholas, the one whose sister got killed, he said it was just a building."

Teddy gave a slight shudder.

"I'd hate to see some place where a murder actually happened, I don't mean in Victorian times or like that, but where someone you knew got killed. It must be awful." She stopped suddenly and bit her lip. "I mean..."

Carlos looked back at her, his expression bleak. Aubrey knew what he was thinking. The scene of a murder was what he actually had seen, and so had Aubrey. Carlos's mother had been lying on her bed in their cheerless little flat, one sparkly flip-flopped foot hanging over the edge. Her eyes had been wide open, staring up at the ceiling, and a large purple bruise stained down into her oddly-angled neck. She had looked like a broken puppet.

Apart from the person who had killed her, Carlos had been the first to witness the scene. He still had, Aubrey knew, nightmares about it. Nightmares from which he woke sweating and terrified and he would reach for Aubrey for comfort. He'd lie, muttering into the warm furry neck the details of scenes in which his feet had stuck to the floor and he was unable to reach her, scenes in which he ran and ran until at last reaching a door he pushed it open, panting and breathless, only to discover another door and after that another until at last he had found himself back at the beginning and staring down at his mother's lifeless body. The nightmares came less frequently now but they hadn't entirely disappeared.

"I'm sorry, Carlos," said Teddy, her expression contrite. "I wasn't thinking. I didn't mean..."

Carlos smiled.

"It's all right," he said. Although it wasn't all right. It would never be all right, but that wasn't Teddy's fault.

"Anyway, that Nicholas bloke said it was okay in the end. Like, it wasn't anything to be frightened of."

Teddy nodded, her expression thoughtful.

"I expect that's the best way to think about it. Because really, when you think about it, everybody has to die somewhere."

For a moment, Teddy and Carlos fell silent while they tried

and failed to grapple with the impossible concept of either of them ever actually getting old, never mind dying.

"Oh, get lost, Casper!" Teddy turned her head as her younger brother crept up behind her and placed a fake plastic spider on her neck. She flicked it away and turned back to Carlos. "Sorry, it's just Casper being an arse as usual."

Casper's face suddenly filled the screen, his mouth pulled into a wide grimace by his forefingers and his eyes rolling upwards. He spoke in a deep gruff voice.

"Hello, Carlos."

Carlos laughed. You couldn't feel down for too long when Casper was around. He had been the scourge of every school that had the misfortune to count him among their number, and all of them had expelled him. He was nevertheless impossible to dislike.

"Hello, Casper."

Casper squeezed himself in next to Teddy, ignoring her attempt to shove him away.

"I know all about this murder thing that you've been talking to Teddy about," he said.

Teddy turned and glared at him.

"Only because you've been listening at doors again. I'm telling Mum. You've got to stop doing that."

Casper grinned.

"I've come to offer the services of the Casper Beaumont International Detective Agency."

Carlos tried to keep a straight face. The Casper Beaumont International Detective Agency had been, without his parents' knowledge, set up in their summer house the previous summer, complete with several laptops and a clock that showed the different times in various parts of the world. Whether it had actually done any detecting so far was unknown.

"Thank you, Casper," said Carlos gravely.

He had been about to say, 'but no thank you.' But then he paused.

When Jeremy, Mike and Nicholas had come home earlier he had been slightly dreading seeing them. Well, not Jeremy and Mike but Nicholas. Because Nicholas was a member of the same club as him. The club that nobody wanted to join. The club whose only membership requirement was that a loved one had met a sudden and violent death. But he had been surprised. Far from creeping in through the door with the cloak of death draped around him, Nicholas had been perfectly cheerful. He had not been downcast. He had not been silent and withdrawn. He had seemed, in a strange way, peaceful.

After her funeral, Carlos had never been back to the place where his mother had died, it had never occurred to him. Would it have made a difference, he wondered, if he had? Would he have been able to erase the indelible image of her broken body and see instead just a room? It was possible, he supposed, although he felt disinclined to try it. In any event, presumably there were other people living there now and they probably wouldn't want him turning up and reminding them of the grim event that had occurred in their home. But from somewhere within him, he felt a need to help Nicholas. A sort of show of solidarity. And now he thought about it, Casper might actually be useful.

Although Casper's school results, when he attended, were appalling, that was only indicative of the fact that he rarely paid any attention in lessons. He preferred to stare out of the windows or continue writing his detective novel, for which he had already written the reviews that would assure its bestseller status.

The last time he had bothered to turn up for an examination, he had whiled away the time by sketching out the manifesto for the political party he was going to form as soon as he was old enough to vote. Not surprisingly, given that the exam was Physics, he had scored precisely zero. But in fact, as almost every despairing teacher had said to his parents, he had a very good brain, he was just selective as to how and where he used it. He was, as one had said with a wry smile, an original thinker. And it was true, there was no denying that Casper had a very different way of looking at things.

Carlos looked at Casper's bright, cheerful face and considered it. Casper might just stumble across something that could be useful to Nicholas. He couldn't do any harm, anyway. Probably.

"Actually, Casper, there might be something you could do."

Casper leaned forward, interested. He pulled a biro out from behind his ear.

"What?"

"Maybe do some research? You know, dig about a bit? There's loads of old stories about it in the newspapers and online. Maybe see if you can find something that nobody's thought about?"

Teddy and Casper turned their heads at the sound of a voice drifting up the stairs. Teddy turned back to the screen.

"That's Mum. We're supposed to be going out today. Got to go. Call you later."

Pushing Casper off the chair, Teddy logged off.

***

Carlos lay stretched out on his bed, Aubrey tucked in beside him. He had a bit of coursework to do, but he'd nearly finished it, he could do it later. Digging down into his jeans pocket, he pulled out his phone and held it aloft. He'd been meaning for ages to sort out his photographs and now would be a good time to do it.

He began scrolling through the images. Some of them were rubbish, but some of them were worth uploading to his laptop, and he could make a file of them and send it to Teddy. There was a great one of Jeremy standing by his car looking grumpy. It must have been that time a few months back when it wouldn't start. Not surprisingly as Jeremy routinely forgot to have it serviced. Jeremy was supposed to be at a meeting. It had turned out all right though. Jeremy had cancelled the meeting and gone and played golf instead.

He smiled. Definitely one to keep. And here was one of Teddy, taken at a cricket match last summer. He felt his heart turn over at the sight of her. She just looked so lovely in her light summer dress, with the daisy chain she had made plaited through her hair. He had taken several photos of her that day and had even printed and placed one of them in a frame which stood on his chest of drawers. He continued scrolling and then stopped. Peering down at the screen he frowned. He didn't remember taking this picture.

He looked at the date. It was recent and taken the day he had visited the churchyard to lay flowers on the murdered policeman's grave. Failing to find it, it had been Teddy who had suggested they donate the flowers elsewhere. Afterwards, he had taken a number of pictures of the churchyard and sent them to her, including the grave that he had eventually laid the flowers on.

He had sent the pictures almost immediately afterwards and he hadn't particularly looked at them. Some of them had been long shots, he had held the phone camera up high and swept around the terrain, some of them were close-up. This one was a long shot, taking in the far side of the churchyard. But he could swear that he had been alone that day. He was sure that there hadn't been anyone else around. But there, unmistakeably, was the figure of a woman. And she was laying flowers on a grave.

He shivered suddenly. Was she a ghost? And then he smiled. No, she was real enough. While a churchyard might be the natural habitat of a ghost, presumably they didn't wear sensible raincoats and carry umbrellas. Nor did they have a large handbag slung over one arm. She was doing what normal people did in a churchyard, what he in fact himself had been doing. She was simply laying flowers, he just hadn't noticed her, that was all.

He brought the screen up closer to his face and enlarged the picture. His eyes opened wider. Those, surely, were the graves of the murdered children. He had seen them that day with Jeremy. They were grouped together and set slightly apart from the other graves. In the picture he could see the distinctive black shiny headstones. He swiped to the next image. There she was again.

He sat up and swung his legs off the bed. Was it significant? He knew that somebody had laid flowers on the children's graves before. Their shrivelled and dried remains had still been there when he and Jeremy had seen them but she wasn't a relation of Nicholas, he was certain. Jeremy had told him that Nicholas only had some old uncle left and this was a woman. Quite an elderly woman. Perhaps it was somebody who had something to do with one of the other children. He raised his head as from outside he heard the sound of car engines starting. Mike and Nicholas must be leaving. He glanced down at the pictures again and then swung his legs off the bed. He'd show the pictures to Jeremy.

***

Jeremy looked up from loading the dishwasher.

"Hello, Carlos. Finished your coursework?"

Carlos strolled over and pulled back a chair. He laid his phone down on the table, screen upwards.

"Nearly," he said. "I was just going through some of my photos. And I found this. It's probably nothing, but I thought you might be interested."

Picking up the phone again, he held it aloft to show Jeremy. "You know when I took some flowers to that policeman's grave?"

Jeremy closed the dishwasher door and sat down. "Yes. What about it?"

"I took some pictures to send Teddy. Look."

Carlos passed the phone to Jeremy.

"But surely, those are the children's graves?"

Carlos nodded. "That's what I thought. Hold on, I'll make the picture bigger."

Obligingly Carlos enlarged the image. A side view of the woman was now clearly visible as she bent over the grave, her hands arranging the flowers in a small vase.

"There's more," said Carlos, and flicked the screen to the next image.

The woman, straightened up now, was looking into the distance, her face expressionless. She was clearly unaware that her image had just been captured on camera.

CHAPTER THIRTY

Jeremy and Aubrey watched from the window of Jeremy's study as a smart red car with the logo of one of the town's estate agents emblazoned on the side pulled up outside the late Mrs Ross's house. A tall young man in a shiny suit and highly polished pointed shoes climbed out and strolled confidently up the garden path. Fishing a key from his pocket he let himself in.

Presumably the property was going on the market and they would soon have new neighbours. Molly had rung to say that she was going shopping after work but he'd tell her when she came home. He cast his eye over the house. From the outside it looked as though it would need some updating. In fact, it looked pretty much the same as it had all those years ago when the photographs had appeared on the front of almost every newspaper.

It hadn't taken much to work out that their erstwhile neighbour, old Mrs Ross, had been the mother of one of the golf course victims. Apart from the fact that Molly had already told him that her daughter had been murdered, Ruth Ross was alliteratively memorable. There were unlikely to have been two in the town. And even less likely that they had both been murdered.

He stared down at the house in which Mrs Ross had lived for so long after her daughter had died. A mirror image of their own, with large bay windows and neat front path, it stood across the street as part of a neat Edwardian row of semi-detached properties and was one of the first things he saw when he drew back the curtains in the morning. How strange to think that Ruth had lived there, that she had looked out of those windows, played in that garden.

Jeremy turned away and felt in his pocket for his phone. Nothing. He'd left several messages on Mike's mobile after seeing the pictures that Carlos had shown him but Mike hadn't got back yet. He hadn't, however, contacted Nicholas. Some instinct told him that it would be a better idea to talk things over with Mike first before setting any hares running. Nicholas had appeared perfectly calm over lunch but who knew how he was feeling now?

What he'd done was a big thing. It might well take a while for it to sink in properly and he would probably appreciate some time on his own. Anyway, the pictures might have a perfectly innocent explanation. In fact, they probably did. Nicholas had told him that she had been their family doctor's wife, so she did have a connection with the family. And why shouldn't she leave flowers? But then again, why would she? Especially after all these years. He could understand it if, in the months immediately following the murders, she had felt moved to leave a tribute to the children. It was a small town and she probably wouldn't have been the only one. It wasn't unknown for complete strangers to leave floral tributes when there had been a tragedy. But surely not decades later.

He turned the thought over as he sought for a rational explanation. What reason would a person have for regularly visiting the graves of three people, two of whom she didn't even have a connection to? Particularly as the deaths had occurred so long ago.

Perhaps the recent talk of the golf course murders had stirred her memory and prompted her to do it. It was possible. But when he had seen the graves with Carlos, there had been the remains of flowers on them then, which indicated that they had been there before the talk of the murders came up in the evening class. That was, of course, assuming that the same person was regularly leaving flowers...

He looked up and smiled as Carlos put his head round the door.

"Are you busy?"

Jeremy shook his head.

"No, not really. I should be but..." He shrugged. Lifting Aubrey from the windowsill, he crossed the room and sat down in one of the little easy chairs. "Come on in."

"Only," said Carlos, sitting down opposite him, "I was just starting my coursework again when I had an email from Casper."

"And what did Casper have to say?" asked Jeremy, settling Aubrey on his lap and running his hand across his back.

"Well, I hope you don't mind, but I talked to Teddy about the golf course murders."

"Don't tell me," said Jeremy. "Casper was listening in. It doesn't matter. It's not a secret."

"That's what I thought. I mean, it's not like nobody knows about it or anything."

It wouldn't matter if they did or they didn't, thought Aubrey. The chances of Carlos not telling Teddy everything were roughly nil, as were the chances of Casper not eavesdropping on anything that sounded interesting. Not that he disapproved of eavesdropping. It was something that he did regularly, as did most cats. How else would they know when to make themselves scarce when a visit to the vet or a stay in the cattery was imminent?

At the thought of the vet, he felt a faint flutter of panic. Having noticed that Vincent was off his food, Molly had taken him to the vet earlier today. What had worried Aubrey was that Vincent hadn't even put up a token protest. He had simply climbed into his basket and flopped down. But they seemed to have been gone an awfully long time.

He squeezed his eyes shut for a moment. The thing that he dreaded the most, the thing that he couldn't bear to contemplate, was the prospect of Molly returning home with an empty cat basket. He pushed the image away and opened his eyes again.

"Anyway," continued Carlos, "Casper's been doing some research and he's had an idea."

Jeremy sat forward and looked interested. When Casper had an idea it was usually worth listening to, if only for the entertainment value.

"An idea about the murders?"

"Yes. He said, what about the weapon? The one that killed the little boy."

Jeremy sat back again.

"What about it? The police never worked out quite what it was and it was never found."

"That's the point," said Carlos, his tone eager. "Casper says that it must have been something unusual. Well, not something that you'd come across every day anyway, and that the murderer couldn't afford to let it be found because it would be linked to him. And if it was never found then it must be hidden or got rid of in some way."

"Well done, Casper. Brilliant deduction." The sarcasm was lost on Carlos who simply nodded.

"I mean, even if you, like, chucked it in a river or something, it might still be found one day. Because sometimes rivers dry up and that. Like when there's a heatwave or something. Or a fisherman or someone swimming might find it."

Jeremy thought about it for a moment.

"True. So where does that take us?"

"Well, Casper reckons it's probably buried somewhere. But not, like, in a back garden or anything because people move house and build extensions and that. Casper says that if the police never worked out what it was or where it was hidden, then it's in an obvious place. Somewhere that nobody would think to look, somewhere that nobody would go digging."

"Which is?"

"The churchyard. Casper says that it's in a grave."

"In a grave?"

Carlos nodded.

"Casper says that it could have just been sort of pushed in the ground. Which would be easy if it was like a knife or something."

"Carlos," Jeremy spoke patiently, "do you realise how many graves there are in the churchyard? Do you think that the vicar is going to let them all be dug up on the off-chance that a murder weapon from years ago might be found? I shouldn't think that any surviving relatives would be too pleased, either."

"You wouldn't have to dig up all of them," said Carlos. "Casper says that when someone hides something, it's never just random. There's always, like, a connection. Even if the person hiding it doesn't know it. It's the same with numbers. People never just choose random numbers. It's all about being subconscious and that."

Carlos paused. He hadn't quite understood this point but he was sure that Jeremy would. Jeremy looked interested.

"And what's the connection in this case?"

"Casper says that it's most likely that the weapon is buried in a grave with the same name or initials of the murderer or the same birthday. Because of the subconscious thing."

Jeremy laughed.

"Which would be fine. If we knew the name or the initials of the murderer, or indeed when his birthday was. We're going round in circles a bit here, Carlos."

Carlos looked crestfallen.

"Oh. Right."

Although, thought Jeremy, Casper actually had a very good point. Nothing was ever really random. When people chose lottery numbers there was always some connection, the birthdate of a loved one or a significant anniversary, some numbers which had some meaning for them. Which was why when he remembered to buy a lottery ticket he always bought a lucky dip. Because he knew that once he chose a set of numbers he'd have to stick with them forever and he'd have to buy a ticket every week. Because, for sure, the one week that he didn't buy a ticket with those numbers it would come up a winner.

But the point still held about the number of graves. Even in the unlikely event that they could persuade the police that that was where the murder weapon would be found, he couldn't imagine they would have the time or resources to undertake such an operation. In any event, he had the feeling that permission from the Home Office or the Minister for Justice or something had to be given to exhume a grave. You couldn't just go around digging people up.

He stood up at the sound of a car on the drive. Molly was back earlier than he had expected. He glanced out of the window. It was Mike. Jeremy raced downstairs, followed by Carlos. Aubrey chased after them. He didn't know what was happening but it seemed like it might be something exciting. He hadn't often seen Jeremy move that quickly.

"What is it?" Jeremy asked, pulling the front door open. "Has something happened?"

"You could say that," said Mike, as Jeremy ushered him through to the sitting room. "I got home and realised that I hadn't got my phone. It wasn't in the car so I thought that I must have dropped it up at the golf course."

Carlos looked aghast, all thoughts of the golf course murders momentarily driven from his mind.

"Did you find it?"

Aubrey looked at him affectionately. Losing phones was a serious business, he knew. Carlos was practically welded to his, and Molly and Jeremy were nearly as bad. None of them went anywhere without their phones being in reaching distance. He'd sat on Molly's once when it was left lying on the windowsill. It was only when it started ringing that she found it. He wasn't sure who had been more startled, him or Molly.

Mike nodded.

"Somebody picked it up in the car park and handed it in to the office. It must have fallen out of my pocket when I got out of the car. Anyway, while I was there I ran into Tracey, the policewoman that I told you about. The one that works on the cold cases. She had news."

"Have there been some developments?" asked Jeremy.

Mike nodded and sat down.

"It's the DNA match. The one that Margaret was talking about on her podcast."

"What about it?"

"It's familial," said Mike.

Carlos looked at him, bewildered.

"What does familial mean?"

"It means closely connected to somebody else," said Mike. "A member of the same family. According to Tracey somebody has come into the system whose DNA is a close match with the original DNA from the scene of the murder. Which means that it's almost certainly a close relative."

"Who is it?" Jeremy caught his breath. "Did she tell you?"

"A bloke called Jack Bellingham. He was pulled over for drunk driving on his way back from a business lunch."

"Who's the close relative? Does Tracey know?"

"She didn't know for sure but the most likely is his father. Dr Raymond Bellingham. Helen Bellingham's late husband."

CHAPTER THIRTY-ONE

Helen watched from the window as the men climbed out of the car. They might be in plain clothes, but they had police stamped all over them. There was no mistaking that air of quiet authority. Besides, who else wore suits and travelled in pairs apart from Jehovah's Witnesses? And these two didn't look like they were coming to ask her if she'd thought about Jesus lately. She supposed that she could pretend to be out, but they'd only come back later.

She felt suddenly calm. She had known this was coming from the moment that Anna had WhatsApped her last night and, among other things, told her about Jack's arrest and his outrage at having his DNA taken. Anna had more or less just mentioned it in passing, an add-on to all the other family news. She had stood there listening in appalled silence to her daughter's pleasant voice as it casually dropped the bombshell that was almost certain to shatter all their lives.

Of the many scenarios she had imagined over the years, she had never foreseen this one. That there might eventually emerge something that would link Raymond to the murders she had known about. That it might come through his son had never occurred to her. The memory of that terrible evening all those years ago, so long locked away, washed over her like icy rain as the taller of the two officers paused and murmured something to his colleague before opening the gate and striding up the garden path.

It had been late afternoon and the children had been upstairs in their bedrooms doing their homework. She had been doing the ironing in the kitchen, an ordinary everyday chore and one which normally she quite liked. But that day, even the warm smell of freshly ironed laundry had failed to soothe her. From the time she had woken up that morning, she had felt the pressure building. It had been straining inside her, building up to the point where she could hardly breathe. It had been triggered, she knew, by a report on television the previous evening. It had been the anniversary of the golf course murders and the local station had reported on the fact.

That afternoon she had stood, iron in one hand, as she heard the click of the front door. He had gone straight to his study. Some instinct, to this day she didn't really know what, had made her put the iron down, unplug it, and follow him. Normally she would never have gone into his study without knocking, but that day she did. She had closed the door behind her, standing with her back to it. He'd looked up from his desk and eyed her in stony-faced silence. Her voice, when it came, was surprisingly calm.

"I know it was you."

The words hung between them. He had regarded her, those features that she had once thought so attractive, now appeared dissipated and corrupt. The broken veins around his nose, a result of drinking too much whisky, seemed more noticeable with every passing week. He had reached across his desk and picked up his fountain pen. She watched as his slim fingers began fiddling with it, unscrewing the cap and screwing it back on again. While once she had ached with longing at the thought of those long fingers touching her, now her skin crawled at the thought of it.

"What was me?"

His voice was measured and steady, his eyes hard. She had once read that when under pressure, the best tactic is to answer a question with a question. It throws the other party off balance and forces them on to the back foot. Apparently it was called the litigator's technique. Whatever it was called, he had it down to a fine art.

"Those children. I know that you had something to do with it."

"Did I?"

He had got up suddenly and walked across to the window, standing with his back to her. She had followed him and tugged violently at his sleeve.

"Just tell me. I need to know."

And she had. She had needed to know. He spun round and pushed her away, the flat of his hand hard against her shoulder. She staggered back and steadied herself against the edge of the desk.

"And what good would that do you? What are you going to do? Go to the police?"

He sat back down at his desk and smiled, a thin cracking of the lips that showed the lines around his mouth. She stared at him, suddenly terrified. What on earth was she thinking? Why hadn't she just stayed quiet? By forcing him out into the open she would achieve nothing. In fact, far from achieving anything she was actively putting herself in jeopardy. Her mouth had gone dry and she looked instinctively towards the door. He stood up again and moved towards her.

"Sit down."

He pointed towards one of the two little easy chairs that

stood either side of the fireplace and she stumbled unwillingly towards it. Seating himself opposite her, he leaned forward, hands clasped loosely between his knees.

He was, she suddenly knew, going to make her complicit. Always at least ten steps ahead of her, he was going to draw her into his web by telling her what he had done. She had been a fool to confront him. For as long as she didn't know for sure, then she wasn't involved. She couldn't be accused of anything and nobody could blame her. She felt her heartbeat quicken as he tipped his head to one side and regarded her through narrowed eyes as though assessing exactly how stupid she was.

Suddenly, he reached forward and grasped her by the wrist, twisting her body forward and forcing her to look at him. She remained silent but unable to look away. Now the irresistible urge to learn the truth shivered and dissolved. She didn't want to know what he had done. She wanted to turn the clock back, just by an hour, and be back in the kitchen, away from him and safely doing the ironing. He dropped her wrist and sat back.

"All right. You want to know. I'll tell you. They saw me," he said flatly. "The air raid shelter was where Charles and I would meet."

Charles. The name of the person he had written about in his diary. The name of the handsome young man in the photographs. The lithe naked young man with the sparkling eyes and thick shoulder-length hair. The man who her husband had wanted more than her. From the sitting room she had heard the sound of the television being switched on. One of the children had finished their homework. The opening music of a daily soap opera played, the familiar notes drifting softly across the hall. He began speaking again, his voice low.

"We chose the shelter because we thought that nobody ever went down there. We couldn't go to a hotel, one of us might have been recognised. I couldn't go to his house, he still lived with his parents. He came here once or twice when you were out but it was too risky. The shelter was perfect. It was so overgrown that most people would have forgotten it had been built, if they ever knew in the first place."

He looked at her, his dark eyes fathomless, as he continued.

"Afterwards, we would always leave separately. Just in case somebody spotted us and wondered what we were doing. I don't suppose that was really necessary but it was always better to err on the side of caution. That day, when he'd gone, I was just tidying myself up when I heard a rustle from the corner. At first I thought it was some kind of rodent. And then it came again, a scuffling sound. Louder. And I knew we hadn't been alone. I walked towards the noise and there they were. Two faces looking back at me. They were right in the far corner, they'd made a little den down there."

At last she had found her voice.

"What did you do?"

She had, she knew, been hoping from somewhere deep within herself that there could still be some sort of plausible explanation. That he could convince her that there had been some justification for his appalling acts.

"I recognised one of them." His voice sounded almost conversational, as though he were telling her about an old friend that he had unexpectedly run into. "I was their family doctor. I was about to tell them some story, explain that Charles had been taken ill and I was helping him. Something like that. And then she spoke to me."

"What did she say?"

Her voice sounded harsh, her throat dry. She would have given anything not to have started this but it was too late now. There was no turning back.

"She said that they had seen us down there before. That was all. Just that they had seen us down there before." He paused and then continued. "They started to move towards the steps leading out. And then I just grabbed them. Both of them. It wasn't difficult. They couldn't have weighed more than about eight stone between them. Afterwards, I pulled them back into the shelter as far as I could. I couldn't take the risk of moving them somewhere else, but I reasoned that with a bit of luck it would be some time before anybody found them. And I was right," he added.

She watched as he got up and poured himself a whisky from the decanter that stood on his desk. He cradled the glass in his hand for a moment before lifting it to his mouth.

"I don't think that you quite understand, Helen." His brow beetled into a frown as he spoke. "I had to keep them quiet. I couldn't allow them to talk."

He sounded impatient, as though trying to explain some perfectly obvious fact to a recalcitrant child. And she had suddenly understood him. For the first time she had understood the very essence of his nature. To him, other people were simply accessories to his life. They were useful or not useful. She had been useful. By marrying him, she had not only provided him with children, but she had also provided him with the perfect cover. His first wife had, presumably, ceased to be useful. Perhaps she had demanded more from him than he was prepared to give her, and so he had discarded her. He was absolutely at the centre of his own universe and other people were largely irrelevant. The children in the air raid shelter had been no more to him than irritating flies to be swatted. He had taken no pleasure in harming them, he had simply dispatched them. His next words chilled her to her very bones.

"So you see, obviously, I had to shut them up. One careless word and I would have been ruined. We both would have been ruined. We would have lost everything."

She had stared at him, appalled as the slow acceptance of

what he was saying seeped through her. Raymond was a well-respected professional man. He had considerable standing in the neighbourhood. He was the doctor who regularly sat on the board of local charities, the married doctor who insisted that his family attend Sunday service at their local church with him, the doctor who could be relied on to turn out in the night to attend to a sick patient. The fact that he did these things to enhance his own feeling of superiority was by the by. The fact was, he did them and he was respected for it. What would his patients think if they knew of the double life that he led? He, and many of his patients, had been born at a time when to be gay was a crime for which a man could be sent to prison, and there were, undoubtedly, some people in the town who thought that the law should never have been changed.

"And there were our children to consider," he had added. "Think of the effect on them."

And then she was lost, as he knew she would be. For whatever he was, whatever he had done, she could not and would not let the children pay the smallest price for it.

"And Charles?" she asked eventually. "What happened to him?"

"He left home and moved to another town," he said flatly. "I never saw him again."

"But there have been others?"

"Yes."

She felt suddenly, inexpressibly weary. A wave of fatigue swept through her and she had longed to just lie down and close her eyes. Instead, she forced herself to continue. As her mother used to say, in for a penny, in for a pound. She'd come this far, it was better to see it through it now, to rip the plaster off and take the pain in one hit so that there were no more unanswered questions to torment herself with. She had drawn a deep breath and steeled herself.

"What about the boy? What about Tommy?"

His face had hardened still further.

"What about him?"

There it was again. The litigator's technique.

"He wasn't in the shelter."

He had, she could tell, momentarily played with the idea of denying any responsibility, but then changed his mind. No matter how stupid he thought her, presumably even she could doubt the possibility of two child murderers operating in the town at the same time.

"No, he was outside. He'd been looking for lost golf balls to sell back to the club members. He knew about the shelter and he saw both Charles and me come out. He knew who I was, he used to deliver our newspapers. Later, when the police found the girls he put two and two together. And made precisely four."

He begun to pace around the room, taking short determined strides, his brow furrowed and his hands deep in his pockets. She remained silent as he began speaking again.

"He came here when you were out. It was a Saturday and you were taking the children somewhere, he must have watched you leave. The little bastard knocked on the door and said that he had something interesting to tell me. And then he tried to blackmail me. Said that he would go to the police unless I gave him fifty pounds." Raymond had sneered suddenly. "Fifty pounds. Typical lack of ambition of that type of boy. But it might as well have been fifty thousand, because I had no intention of giving it to him. He stood there, with a stupid smirk on his face, as if he had me exactly where he wanted. I suspect it wasn't the first time he'd tried his hand at a spot of blackmail. It was very practiced."

That, she thought, might very well be true. Newspaper boys and girls had good reason to be on other peoples' properties and who knew what they saw and heard as they went about their deliveries.

"Anyway," Raymond continued, "I let him talk for a bit while I thought about it. I came to the conclusion that even if the police didn't believe him, which, let's be honest, was the most likely outcome, it might still plant the seed of an idea. At the very least, they would have to ask some questions. And I couldn't afford for that to happen."

He looked directly at her, his eyes hard. "He was hardly a loss to the world. You didn't like him yourself, you told me so."

No, she thought, she hadn't liked him. He was a nasty, prying little boy who always looked as though he knew more than was good for him. And on this occasion he had. But he didn't deserve to die.

"I stuffed him in my golf bag, he wasn't very big, and put it in the boot of my car until it was dark. His legs stuck out of the bag a bit but it didn't matter. I just put my clubs around them."

And he'd looked across at her, eyebrows raised, expectant, as if he seriously wanted some kind of response. She simply stared back.

"I had all day to think about what to do with him. I thought about burying him in the garden at first, but that would have been too risky. Anybody might have seen me. Anyway, I didn't want to mess up the garden."

She had looked at him, appalled.

"I decided in the end that I would take him to the golf club. I thought I'd drop him off round the back by the bins. It was the weekend, nobody would go round there until at least Monday or Tuesday and if I pushed him to the far corner even then they might not notice him. It was dark, it was unlikely that anybody would see me. And they didn't."

She felt suddenly sick. His tone had been completely casual. He talked as if he'd had a slight problem but had sorted it out with a bit of lateral thinking, for which he should be congratulated. And all the time, on that day she had been making dinner, talking to the children, doing all the housewifely things that she normally did, Tommy's poor little broken body had been outside, crunched up in a golf bag.

Raymond stopped pacing and faced her. She had found herself struggling to resist the urge to put up her hand and ask his permission to leave. As if reading her mind, he had strolled towards the door and pulled it open.

"And now, Helen, we will never speak of this again."

And they never did.

CHAPTER THIRTY-TWO

Aubrey wrapped his tail around himself and watched from the windowsill as Carlos and Rubble busied themselves in the kitchen, Carlos frequently returning to the notes he had pinned to the fridge with a magnet. They were, he knew, cooking a special meal for Molly and Jeremy as practice for a test that they had to take in the college training restaurant where they would be cooking for college governors.

Mike and Nicholas had been invited to the practice meal too, so today they would be eating in the dining room rather than the kitchen with, as Carlos had told him, a proper tablecloth and everything. Aubrey wasn't quite sure what the everything was, in fact, he wasn't quite sure what a tablecloth was, but it sounded good. Next to him lay Vincent, his sleek dark body stretched out, his eyes tight shut.

Aubrey moved slightly to give him more room. Vincent might have lost some weight lately but he was still a big cat. He eyed him affectionately. When Molly had returned from the vet he had intended to race out and meet her, but his legs felt stuck to the floor and he had found himself unable to move. Instead, he had sat by the back door, heart in mouth, as he waited for her to come in. When he had spotted the distinctively Vincent shape in the cat basket the relief had been overwhelming. All cat lives come to an end, they both knew that better than most, but he wasn't ready to let Vincent go just yet.

It was a measure of how serious the situation had been, that not only had Vincent been prescribed some tablets to take, but he was actually taking them instead of holding them in his mouth and then quietly spitting them out when Molly was out of sight.

He glanced out of the window at the sound of car doors shutting.

"Rubble." Carlos looked up from the oven where he'd been adjusting the temperature. "Get the menu cards, quick. They're here."

Nicholas gave a sigh of contentment and stood up.

"Shall I give them a hand clearing?"

Jeremy grinned.

"No, sit down. That's part of the test."

As if on cue, Carlos and Rubble entered the dining room, Rubble with a tea towel neatly folded over his arm and Carlos bearing a pot of coffee.

"Was it all right?" Carlos sounded anxious as he placed the coffee on the table. "I mean, like, did we pass?"

"Of course you passed," said Molly, handing him the completed score card which he and Rubble had carefully prepared. "It was fantastic."

"Come and sit with us," said Jeremy. "You've earned a rest. We can sort this lot out later."

Carlos and Rubble grinned at each other and sat down.

Carlos looked across at Mike.

"Has anything else happened? Like with that family stuff?"

Mike looked puzzled.

"What family stuff?"

"He means familial," said Jeremy. He turned to Carlos.

"According to Mike, the police have visited Helen Bellingham. He heard it from his friend Tracey. Who he ran into this morning." Jeremy gave a slight grin and raised his eyebrows. "You seem to be running into Tracey an awful lot."

Mike coloured slightly and poured himself some coffee.

"That Mrs Bellingham, she's saying that she doesn't know anything about it," said Rubble.

Jeremy looked at him, astonished.

"How on earth do you know that?" he asked.

"My aunt, the one that was working at the college, the new job she got was with the police, like doing office work and that. She typed up the interview notes. I heard her telling my mum about it, and then I heard my mum telling the receptionist that works at our hotel."

"Why didn't you tell us?" demanded Carlos.

"I forgot," said Rubble simply, and beamed round the table.

Jeremy suppressed the urge to ask him if he could get access to the notes. While printing out a college register might, just about, err on the side of acceptability, pinching a set of police notes most certainly wouldn't be. However, if Rubble just happened to remember the contents of the interview, even in broad terms... He turned to Rubble.

"Rubble, I don't suppose you can remember what your aunt told your mum?"

Rubble nodded.

"She said that Mrs Bellingham told the police she didn't know anything about it. My aunt said that she was in total denial. What does that mean?" he added, his face bewildered.

"It means that she's completely refusing to accept that her husband might have done anything wrong," said Jeremy.

Rubble nodded again, and looked thoughtful.

"Well, she would, wouldn't she?"

He looked confused as Molly, Jeremy, Mike and Nicholas burst out laughing. What was so funny about that?

"My aunt told my mum that the police haven't got any real proof," continued Rubble.

Mike nodded. "She's right. The fact that the DNA was found doesn't necessarily mean that he was the murderer. According to Tracey," he coloured again slightly, "the police are going to need more. Even though they may be pretty sure that Bellingham is their man and there obviously won't be a trial, they'll still want to put this one to bed. In criminal cases the prosecution have to prove beyond a reasonable doubt that the accused is guilty, and when you think about it, there could be all sorts of reasons why Dr Bellingham's DNA was found on the clothes of the victims. If he was alive the police could simply ask for an explanation and then try to disprove it. As it is, they're probably going to have to come up with something else, something more concrete. It would have been helpful if they had ever found the knife."

"How?" asked Jeremy. "Surely, even if it was somehow connected to him, he would have wiped it clean?"

Mike nodded.

"Definitely. But that was before we knew about DNA. Even a tiny trace might have been caught under or around the handle where it joins the blade."

"What about the girls' clothing?" asked Molly. "How could he have explained his DNA being on those?"

"Well, he could have run into the girls earlier in the day. One of them might have fallen over for example and he stopped to help. He was a doctor, after all. When you put your mind to it, there could be any number of perfectly plausible reasons. The problem is that there's no way of knowing. It was all so long ago. Really, they need something more tangible to tie the case up properly. And the chances of getting that now are remote to say the least."

"There's still the attack on Margaret to consider," said Jeremy. "Do the police think it's connected?"

Mike nodded.

"Probably. They're pretty certain that it was Helen Bellingham. But, again, it's finding the proof. Apparently the college CCTV wasn't working so they couldn't get anything there. They can't even work out what the weapon was, just that it was something heavy."

From across the table Nicholas shifted slightly and cleared his throat.

"I wasn't going to mention it, given that this is a social occasion, but as we're already talking about it..."

"What?" asked Mike. "Have you found out something else?"

"I went to see Margaret. I had been intending to visit her the day I ran into Jeremy at the hospital, but I changed my mind. Still, it felt like something that I had to do. I went yesterday."

"How is she?" asked Molly.

"Much better. Apparently she can go home in a few days. She told me that the police had been questioning her about the attack."

Jeremy leaned forward.

"And?"

"The last thing she remembers about that evening is walking to her car, opening the door to put her bag in and then sensing that somebody was standing behind her. After that everything is a blank. The next thing she knew, she was waking up in hospital. One thing she did remember though was the smell of perfume."

Molly looked interested.

"What was it, did she know?"

Nicholas shook his head.

"No. But she said that she'd definitely recognise it again."

Helen glanced down at her mobile. Nothing. She wasn't surprised. It had been silent for two days. News travels fast in a small town and there had been no confirmation from Moira or Diana as to their usual weekly lunch arrangement. Nor had there been any emails suggesting their next stately home visit. She didn't blame them. Not really. Had she been in their shoes she would probably have done the same.

That people were already talking, she knew. She hadn't imagined the sudden frost in the atmosphere when she visited the newsagents this morning. At least she had warned the children though. She had taken her courage in her hands the previous evening and phoned both of them. She had told them what might be coming but had made light of it, stressing that it was just another false lead, some silly idea that a journalist had got hold of and it would blow over. They had been shocked but they had believed her and that was all that mattered. She had to hang on to the thought that the police had no real proof that Raymond was responsible. And he was dead, there could be no trial.

She walked through to the kitchen and looked around her. She had expected to feel more than she did. She thought about it while she waited for the kettle to boil. As long as she held her nerve, and she would, she had nothing to fear. All she had to do was deny. Deny, deny, deny. She had, she felt, shown the right amount of shock when the police had told her about Raymond. She had heard herself stumbling for words in trying to frame a response. It was okay, she'd had time to rehearse. When they had asked if they could search the house, she had willingly agreed. They could search all they liked, they would find nothing to help them.

Thank God she'd burned the diary. At least that part of the whole dreadful business would remain buried. While the police might be sure that Raymond had been involved, she would give them nothing to work on. Not a scrap. Not to protect Raymond, but to protect Anna and Jack. Whatever else happened, she must shield them at all costs. They must not suffer for what their father had done. She was sorry about Margaret, of course she was, and if she could wind the clock back she would, but there was nothing that she could do about it now. She had acted purely from instinct, a moment of absolute madness, the fear and the terror that had been building up in her, the appalling thought that Jack and Anna might find out the truth, had overwhelmed her. But it was clear that the police, suspicious though they might be, had nothing on her or they would have charged her by now.

She hadn't told the children about the police visit and on balance she had decided that she wouldn't. It wouldn't be so bad for Anna, so like her father in terms of self-containment, she would take it on the chin. She would be shocked but she would say very little and carry on as though nothing had happened. It would be Jack that would struggle. She felt her heart give a tiny squeeze as she thought about his large blue-grey eyes and his soft sensitive mouth. Jack had spent his childhood trying to win his father's approval, trying to be the boy that he thought his father wanted him to be and by and large he had succeeded. But it had come at a cost to him, she knew. If he were to find out the truth she wasn't sure that he'd ever get over it.

At least Anna was far away in New Zealand and remote from the immediate impact if the story hit the press. If only Jack were, too. Suddenly she realised that she was looking at the perfect solution to her immediate problems. She would put the house on the market and go to New Zealand. She had sufficient money to rent a small apartment until the money from the house came through and she would be fine. She would be sorry to leave Clara but, while theoretically it was possible to take her with her, she really didn't think that she would survive the journey. Jack would take her, she was sure.

CHAPTER THIRTY-THREE

Jeremy strolled through the churchyard, hands in pockets, and a slight hunch to his shoulders in defence against the chill in the late-afternoon air. Ahead of him, Aubrey and Vincent sauntered through the grass, relaxed and lithe, but eyes sharp. He was glad that he'd decided to come out. The lunch that Carlos and Rubble had cooked had been delicious but he wasn't used to three courses at that time of day. When their guests had left, he had fallen asleep in the armchair, waking to a slightly thick head and a dry mouth.

As he walked, he was conscious of a feeling of deflation. From what Mike had said, it looked unlikely that the late Dr Raymond Bellingham would ever be held to account, not even posthumously. And as long as Helen Bellingham held out, and it was looking very likely that she would, that would be the end of it. There was nothing else to be done. Even a DNA sweep of the air raid shelter was unlikely to uncover anything useful. Apart from the fact that any number of people may have been down there in the years since the murders, there could well be a good reason why Bellingham may have been down there too. So that was that.

He glanced around him, wondering where the cats had got to. It would start to get dark soon and they ought to be getting back home. Glancing over to the area where the old headstones were being removed he caught a glimpse of Vincent as he stalked through the overgrown grass. He walked towards him, rattling his keys and calling as he did so. Aubrey, who had been scrabbling around in the earth, turned and looked up at him.

"What's that, old chap?" Jeremy leaned over. "What have you found?"

There, lying among the newly dug earthworks, lay something that looked like a knife. Broad and flat with a slight bevel, half-buried in the earth softened by the spring rain that had fallen earlier in the day, its antique hilt was set with semi-precious stones. Jeremy picked it up and held it for a moment in the palm of this hand. Across the blade were inscribed some words. Jeremy peered down more closely. 'To dear Doctor James Bellingham, from his grateful patients upon the occasion of his retirement.' Jeremy glanced across at the neat stack of headstones set against the wall and read the inscription on the nearest one.

Here lies the final resting place of Roger Blackstone.
Jeremy smiled. Clever old Casper.

THE END

ALSO BY ALISON O'LEARY

ACKNOWLEDGEMENTS

First, huge thanks and appreciation to the great team at Bloodhound for their professional and friendly approach. It has been a genuine pleasure working with them.

Thanks also to my editor M. Sean Coleman for his expert support and guidance.

Last, but by no means least, thank you to all my lovely readers for joining Aubrey and Vincent on their adventures.

ABOUT THE AUTHOR

I was born in London and spent my teenage years in Hertfordshire where I spent large amounts of time reading novels, watching daytime television and avoiding school.

Failing to gain any qualifications in science whatsoever, the dream of being a forensic scientist collided with reality when a careers teacher suggested that I might like to work in a shop. I don't think she meant Harrods.

Later studying law, I decided to teach rather than go into practice and have spent many years teaching mainly criminal law and criminology to young people and adults.

I enjoy reading crime novels, doing crosswords, and drinking wine. Not necessarily in that order.

A NOTE FROM THE PUBLISHER

Thank you for reading this book. If you enjoyed it please do consider leaving a review on Amazon to help others find it too.

We hate typos. All of our books have been rigorously edited and proofread, but sometimes mistakes do slip through. If you have spotted a typo, please do let us know and we can get it amended within hours.

info@bloodhoundbooks.com